Seaside Tales of Death or Destruction

I0581485

Jane Carmody

Seaside Tales of Death or Destruction

Seaside Tales of Death or Destruction
ISBN 978 1 76109 254 1
Copyright © text Jane Carmody 2022

First published 2022 by
Ginninderra Press
PO Box 3461 Port Adelaide 5015
www.ginninderrapress.com.au

Contents

The Ring of Chains 7

The Visitation 21

Something Red 25

The Lighthouse 27

Clouds 36

Accidental Plot 53

Freya 61

Duncan Trevaniel 67

Leagues 77

Messenger 82

The Ring of Chains

It was a distant howl at first, like the wail of someone grieving. It grew louder and closer. Through the forest it thrashed, beating back the branches. It rushed into the paddocks, lashed and sucked the moisture from the fern-laden gullies and swept past the 'suicide gum' where a worker had swung. Charlotte could hear the chains that were slung over the branch of that tree clanging and rattling. It sent chills up her spine.

She lay in her bed sweating and then felt the slight stir of air around her nostrils as the wind forced a draught through the floorboards, weatherboards and windows. Clattering along like a madman, the wind tossed branches upon the corrugated-iron roof and drummed and rippled under the eaves.

The cotton sheet was pulled up around her ears, but it was no defence against the raucous wind. She crept out of bed and entered the kitchen. As she opened the back kitchen door to the veranda, it was flung back with a jolt, dispersing a harried array of leaves into the room. It displaced the freshly ironed doilies from the homestead that had been neatly placed on the kitchen table.

She feared that the noise would disturb her parents, making them angry to be woken in the middle of the night, especially with the Spencers arriving tomorrow and therefore an early start. For a moment, she stood still and strained to listen for movement in their room above the wind. She braced herself against the door, but she could hear nothing and so she stepped outside as the wind swirled around her light night-dress and flipped back her plaits.

'Paddy, Paddy,' she called into the gusts.

From the shed, a lethargic brown mongrel stepped gingerly onto the ground and shook before sitting to bite a flea.

'Come on, Paddy,' she said, stroking the beast lovingly. 'Come in with me tonight.'

The dog stood at the kitchen door as Charlotte took hold of the handle tightly.

'Come on, come on,' she whispered, beckoning the reluctant dog inside, 'but we must get up early so you won't get caught in here,' she warned. She hopped back into her bed and stroked the dog as it sat beside her until she fell asleep.

'You're a sleepy head this morning,' Charlotte's mother Louisa said without looking up as the child appeared at the kitchen table.

'The wind woke me in the night. I'm tired,' she answered apprehensively, noticing that the dog had already been let out.

But Louisa was too busy ironing for the family in order that they have fresh linen to worry about Charlotte having the dog in her room.

Charlotte saw that some of the doilies were soaking again, having been blown to the dusty floor during the night. 'Do you want me to peg them out?'

'What? Yes,' her mother said distractedly.

Charlotte took the doilies from the bucket.

'Here let me see those,' her mother ordered and inspected them intensely, before dismissing Charlotte to hang them outside. She then continued to iron. Her cream cotton dress clung to her as though it were squeezing her breath out. Sweat bled through the threads at her armpits and back as she laboured for the Spencers. Beads formed above her dry severe lips. Greasy orbs trickled from her temple and spilled upon the heavy ironing board.

Charlotte lingered for a moment too long before Louisa snapped, 'Go on, girl, put them on the line.'

She struggled to hold the door as the wind forced it back, creating a mini maelstrom.

'Shut it, shut it,' her mother cried while holding down the flapping linen.

Charlotte pulled the door shut while firmly holding the doilies. She stepped onto the creaking dry boards of the veranda. The sun had climbed above the surrounding eucalypt forest casting definite shadows upon the paddock. Charlotte noticed the cows clumped together in large black knots.

It was already hot as Charlotte attended to hanging the doilies. The dirt whipped her bare legs and spun into eddies behind the shed. She carefully attached the washing as the linen flicked with resistance upon the line. She could imagine the doilies flying off into the sky, free of constraints, climbing into the heavens and soaring above the rippling paddocks, swaying forests, trembling lakes and sand blasted beaches. She squinted watching the threadbare clouds stretching upon the blue opalescence. The back door opened.

'Stop daydreaming, girl. I need your help up at the house. Get dressed.'

Linen was packed into a lined case and loaded onto the cart along with a tureen of cold meat that her mother had cooked, bread, vegetables, eggs and the carcasses of two chickens. Alexandra, the workhorse, swayed and flicked her tail, quietly enduring tenacious bush flies that crawled into her eyes as the cart was loaded. Normally, Louisa would have walked up the path to the homestead with their load. But it was so hot that she decided to conserve her energy for later when the family arrived, knowing that the ladies might call upon her to help unpack or prepare a meal or do any menial task that they or their long-nosed maid saw fit.

The horse heaved its burden up the hill, scrubbed wet under the harness. Charlotte and her mother were shaken along as the wheels scraped the rutted track. Fraught acacias lining the path tossed their heads as the bracken underskirts snagged. Charlotte's mother confessed her loathing of the heat as she wiped her tangled hair off her forehead, the lines upon her face growing tense as she drew closer to the homestead. She frowned and shielded her eyes as the cart rounded the bend and the dazzling white of the house against the pressing trees seemed to scorch her eyes.

'We will go in through the back, it's more sheltered,' Louisa told Charlotte. 'Be careful handling the tureen. It belongs to the family.'

Shrivelled, quivering petals and leaves, blown down from the climbing rose that grew along the back fence littered the entrance.

'I must sweep them up,' Louisa commented as she opened the door.

Charlotte wondered why. It seemed a thankless task when more would be blown down and swept away in this wind.

To enter the cool, still house brought little relief for Louisa and Charlotte, as they immediately raised sweat making the house ready. The food was put in the cool room. Louisa dusted the tables and charlotte swept the floors. She took off her dusty shoes, not out of respect, but to feel the cool, smooth polished boards under her feet, unlike the rough boards of her own home. She entered Mr and Mrs Spencer's bedroom, where the brocade curtains had been drawn back allowing slanting light to cut across the room. Charlotte gazed into the mirror of the carved oak wardrobe and was entranced by the image. Her straw-coloured hair, although contained in plaits, looked wild and unruly. Hazel eyes gleamed and blushed cheeks were flecked with freckles. She was like a sprite amid the gloomy room with its dark panelled walls and grand mahogany bed. As she swept next to the bed, she saw another image in the bevelled mirror of the dressing table which stood opposite the window. But the characteristics of her face were eclipsed by the backlight.

Next, she entered the bedroom of Clare and Esther, the two Spencer daughters. She was at once confronted by the sumptuous porcelain-faced doll that sat upon Clare's bed. Its impassive vitreous eyes watched as she swished the broom and peeped illicitly into the drawers and fondled tortoiseshell and ivory combs and pins. She glanced back at the imperious doll and then turned away from its knowing stare. A toy pram stood in the corner of the room. Fingering the embroidered coverlet and lace pillow, she successfully managed to displace a folded doll's costume which was hung over the handle. Picking it up from the floor, she noticed the rich quality of the cloth.

Her mother entered the bedroom and leant against the broom, her tousled chignon collapsing down her back, her face shiny and wet, and large dark brown eyes searching. 'What are you doing, miss?'

'The doll's dress fell. Look at it, Mama. Isn't it fancy? I wish I had a dress like that.'

'Wherever would you wear a dress like that, may I ask?'

'I would wear it to…to a fine place – to a tea party. And we would have fresh bread and plum jam, and tea in little china cups with roses on them.'

'Really?'

'And you would be dressed in something even finer, with ribbons and glittering jewels. Like the ones Mrs Spencer owns.'

'Ooh, you little snoop. Glittering jewels? That should be nice. You are such a dreamer, my Charlotte, but you know we could never afford that,' her mother said reflectively as she watched Charlotte for a moment, then ordered her, 'Put that back now, nicely. I don't want the family saying that we spoiled anything in here. I don't want to be owing them nothing. Finish your sweeping so we can go back home.'

Louisa left the room and Charlotte followed, taking one last longing look at the doll.

They walked back along the track that trailed down the hill to their home. They were blown sideways as the wind continued ferociously. Everything looked angled and crooked, disturbed and mean. The door of the shed rattled grimly as the other one banged. In the garden beds surrounding their home, the corn battled back-breakingly to remain upright. The bushes arched like field labourers and the summer flowers were made to sacrifice their fragrant and fragile blooms to the harshness.

From the track, they had a view of the opposite hill. Great draughts of wind drove jagged lines of grass across the paddock. They could make out the figure of Charlotte's father Dan on horseback, with the panting Paddy at his flank crossing toward their home. Charlotte waved, but her father did not respond. She yelled but her voice was overcome by the powerful surges of wind that carried it skyward.

She ran down the hill with her plaits and dress flying, crying out and waving to her father. Then she noticed his arm scratched and bleeding.

'Daddy, Daddy,' she called as she waited at the gate.

Louisa had started to brew some tea by the time Dan and Charlotte entered the house.

'It's hell out there,' Dan said as he sat at the table and threw his hat to the floor.

Louisa frowned at the blasphemy and then noticed his arm. 'What happened? Are you all right?'

'Yes. Yes. Don't fuss. There's a tree blown down near the creek where it runs to the lake and it's pulled some of the fence down. I just got caught up by the broken branches. I'll have to go back down and mend it.'

'What? Now? Please don't do it today,' Louisa implored.

'I have to, Lou. I've put some branches across for now, but it won't last in this wind. Otherwise, those silly beasts will end up getting stuck in the swamp. And I don't want to lose any of 'is lordship's cows.'

'How long will you be? The ferry with the Spencers will be here around eleven.'

'Surely they won't come in this weather.'

'You know they will. They're too mean to spend another night in the lodgings near the station.'

'Well, they'll have to get their own luggage up the hill this time from that bloody pier. I'll be a few hours by the look of it.'

Louisa once again crinkled her brow.

Dan ran his hand through his sandy-coloured hair, sipped his tea from the chipped cup and ate two cakes with icing. 'This is a treat. How come we don't get treats like this when the family aren't here? Aren't we special enough, Mother?' Dan asked, as he winked at Charlotte.

'No, you're not,' Louisa said, exasperated by the heat, fatigue and his flippancy.

She finally sat at the table with Dan and Charlotte, wiped her brow and upper lip with a handkerchief and picked up the cup thoughtfully.

'Come on, Mother, they'll be here and gone before you know it,' Dan comforted.

'It's just they come here and think they're so much better than us. Even that snooty maid – she looks down her pointy nose at me. And they think they're entitled to everything we have.'

'Well, it is their estate – we are only the caretakers.'

'No. You're the one employed as the caretaker, not me. They think they are entitled to everything we have, like my pretty brooch that Miss Edwina borrowed and hasn't given back. And the fish you caught last time that they wanted and we ended up with hardly any. They don't own the lake.'

'Without them, I wouldn't have a job,' Dan said as he got up from the table and kissed Louisa on the cheek.

She shrugged and turned her face crossly. 'You know that's not true,' she shot back.

'I need to go. I'll be back as soon as I can.'

'Can I come with you, Daddy?' Charlotte asked hopefully as she watched him leave.

'Not today, my sweet Charlotte. Mother needs you to help here,' Dan said, looking for acknowledgement from Louisa.

Louisa turned on Charlotte. 'What? You want to leave me all alone with them too, do you?'

Charlotte longed to ride with her father to creek where the cooling water slid into the muddy banks and onward to the shallow lake. She yearned to sit astride and grapple with Silver, her headstrong, little grey pony and watch his twitching ears, and scold him and spur him on. But she would not provoke her mother. It would be Charlotte, not her pony that would be put into harness today. 'I'll stay with you, Mama,' she conceded.

When Dan had left, Louisa remained at the table and held out her hand to Charlotte. 'Come here, dear girl. It's just not a good day to go.

I need you here.' She patted Charlotte's hand. 'You know, I'll be happy to leave this place one day and have our own place and not have to answer to no one,' she reflected.

A little after eleven, the ferry nosed in at the pier, next to Dan's dinghy. Four ladies crossed the gangplank and held their hats. Their satins rustled vexatiously.

Adele Spencer greeted Louisa, saying, 'Where is Mr Kelly?'

'Hello, Mrs Spencer. A tree has knocked a fence down and my husband has gone to mend it.'

'Can't it wait? How are we to get these belongings up? Mr Spencer is not here to help either. He is staying another night in Melbourne on business. I was relying on your husband, but maybe I shouldn't,' she said sharply.

'I have brought the horse to the gate. The cases can be loaded onto the cart. If Mr Kelly doesn't mend the fence, the cattle will get stuck in the creek when the tide…' Louisa began as Mrs Spencer turned away from her and started at a pace up the hill towards the gate, pulling along some of her luggage.

Esther picked up a hatbox. Clare struggled to take up her large case and giggled when she could only drag it along the path.

'Give it here,' ordered Alvira Walsh, their housekeeper.

Clare abandoned the case and ran along the path, kicking grains into the air as she went. The housekeeper picked up the case and handed it to Charlotte.

'Charlotte won't be taking that,' Louisa protested. 'If Miss Clare cannot carry it, how can you be expecting Charlotte to pick it up. She's half her size.'

'Well, your girl being a country girl, I thought that she would be used to heavy work,' she posed waspishly.

'Charlotte, you come here and pick up the small bags,' Louisa ordered Charlotte, ignoring Mrs Walsh.

The housekeeper took the bag and marched into the wind.

Charlotte picked up another bag and followed Clare and Esther, who were battling their skirts as they strutted up the hill. She watched the girls as the brims of their well held hats quavered. She studied the cut of their skirts, the drape and flash of fabric as it swelled and shrunk with great puffs.

Clare stopped to look at the view through a clearing where some trees had toppled. 'It's so pretty. But look at the seas – they're so rough and scary,' she said to Esther, who disregarded her as she walked to the gate, led by her chin.

She peered down the path and waited for Charlotte to catch up. 'I can take one of those bags,' she offered, holding out her soft white hand.

'Thanks, they are heavy. Whatever do you have in them?'

'Just clothes, really. I think. Actually, I don't know. The maid packed them.'

'If I packed all my clothes into a bag, I would be able to pick them up with my little finger. Was it rough on the ferry?'

'Oh yes. Esther thought she was going to be seasick. But Mother said that it would be unbecoming. I told Essie that she was being a baby. And Mrs Walsh disappeared once or twice. But I liked it with the waves coming over the deck.'

'I think I would have liked it too. Papa takes me out in his dinghy sometimes and one time we were caught in a squall and we were nearly tipped out. The boat was quite full of water and we had to bail it out. It was scary but exciting. We didn't tell Mama because she wouldn't have let me go out again.'

'What have you been doing over summer? Do you go out in the boat?'

'Sometimes, but I also go riding on my pony with Papa sometimes.'

'You do?'

'Yes, I ride with him when we have to move the cattle or ride to the neighbours.'

'Does he get angry with you?'

'Angry?'

'Don't you get in the way?'

'I don't think so. He never says that I do.'

'Esther and I have gone to Father's store sometimes and he always gets annoyed because we put our sticky fingers on the merchandise, or so he says. It's good in one way, though, because he usually grows tired of us and makes one of the staff take us to the tea house for cake and lemonade.'

'It sounds wonderful,' Charlotte sighed.

At the top of the hill, they entered the estate by the gate and loaded the cart. Mrs Spencer climbed aboard, along with Esther and Mrs Walsh. Clare and Charlotte ambled along behind. Louisa walked behind them, her eyes trained on the faux crocodile skin hatbox that was placed where she usually sat.

The recklessness of the day inflicted sticks, leaves and grits on the frailty of the figures as they heaved their way up the hill to the house. They sniffed up grime and shielded their eyes from motes. The noise was terrible as the fluctuating pressure forced its way into the canals of their ears.

The homestead offered shelter from the wind but it amplified its cry. In most rooms, the windows shook and rattled the newcomers as they pretended otherwise and busied themselves unpacking their brilliant luggage. The curtains in various rooms were thrown back or drawn according to the state of mind of the occupant.

Mrs Walsh spun around in her domestic realm like a mad queen, swinging pots and stocking cupboards, cleaning where Louisa had already cleaned, fleshing out cold meat, slicing bread, snatching fresh onions and carrots and cucumbers and tomatoes. All the while, her shoulders broadening as the onerous burden of orchestrating the household was placed upon them. Her apron plumped and flared ominously from overheating. She opened the window slightly to alleviate the stifling air in the kitchen against Louisa's advice. Eventually, the low cool air was stirred away as the sweltering air pulsed in.

Charlotte returned home with her mother for lunch. Their plates were laden with bread and cheese. Louisa stabbed at slabs of it. She stuffed the food into her mouth hungrily. Charlotte nibbled daintily and threw bits to the dog when her mother wasn't looking.

'Mama, Clare asked me if I would like to go back to her house and play with the doll after I have my lunch. May I?'

'No.'

'But why?'

The kettle was steaming hard on the fire. In her agitation, Louisa misjudged and burnt herself on the scorching metal. She cursed to herself and raised her hand to her lips, tearing up and reddening.

Charlotte risked asking again. 'Why, Mama?'

Louisa did not answer immediately. She gripped the kettle and pressed it hard into the cast metal of the oven as though she were impressing the circular confines of her life. She gazed upward and spoke deliberately. 'First of all, I will not have you questioning me.' She breathed deeply and narrowed her lips. She set her gaze on Charlotte as her pupils widened. 'But,' she stopped for emphasis, 'if you must know why, I will tell you, Miss. It's because you are not good enough.'

The first lash was swift. Charlotte felt cut. She tried to swallow, but her dry little mouth refused.

'To them, you are nothing. You are there to serve. You are there for their convenience. She asks you because her sister refuses. If anything happens to the doll, you will be blamed. Don't ever forget your station, because, if you do, people like the Spencers take great delight in reminding you where you belong. The less you have to do with them, the less you can be blamed.'

Charlotte momentarily recovered from the words flung from hardened, wounded, world-weary lips. 'But what about Clare? She is my friend, Mama.' Her eyes were wide and the voice timid and tremulous.

Louisa, in a voice that was almost inaudible, warned, 'She is one of them, Charlotte.'

Charlotte wiped her salty cheek and sniffed as she stood by the lake with Paddy. The water was turbid, unlike it had been yesterday when the glossy azure of the lake crept skyward and forever, soft, mellow, calm and predictable. Beyond the lake, she could hear the waves at the entrance, where the white water hissed and spat. The gulls argued and were heaved into turbulent updraughts. The tiny shells clinked and shattered under her feet, but the noise was obliterated by the surf.

She would have to wait to play with the crafty-eyed doll for another time; another world; another era. Access to the world of the Spencers had been denied by invisible locks and chains. Locks and chains forged by the rigid, prejudiced and incomprehensible adult world. A world brutally revealed, inflicting burdens and limitations on the innocence of childhood.

Charlotte poked her feet into the choppy water of the lake. Lacking the certainty of rhythmic waves, the water sloshed and ripped under incessant perturbation. She knelt to manipulate miniature sandbanks to cave in under the duress of the current and the shell people to perish under the weight.

'What's the matter, Paddy?' she cooed as she looked into the dog's eyes.

He shifted his head and rested it on his paws.

'You are the best. I hate people.' She played with his ear, relishing the direct way he pressed against her. 'Let's go up to the lookout point and see if we can see Daddy down by the creek.'

She took the high track along cliff edge as the dog darted off into the undergrowth. Charlotte baulked as a black lizard darted in front of her. Continuing, she climbed higher as the trees thrashed about next to her and sweat squeezed through her pores. She reached the summit, the lookout point where colossal rocks protruded boldly, seemingly ready to tumble as the roots of spindly shrubs cleaved treacherously to cracks in their foundations.

She sat to take a breath and looked out to sea, beyond the lake, to the roaring white caps and dark troughs. She scanned the turbulent entrance. The turquoise lake looked innocuously shallow and pallid in comparison. But through experience, Charlotte knew otherwise.

From the heights, she looked back along the track and across to the pressing forest that bound and overshadowed the estate. It was then that she saw it. Tainting the perfect blue so shatteringly was a mutating mass of smoke.

So truly horrible was the vision that she could hardly breathe. Horror stories of fires engulfing people so swiftly and killing them alarmed her into action.

Back along the track she raced. Gnarly tree roots tripped her. Saplings slapped her. She panted and cried. Her little heart pounded to nearly breaking point. The path felt nightmarishly long. At last the gate. In her turmoil, she fumbled the latch and gave up. She frantically squeezed herself and Paddy through the fence, ripping her dress.

Bursting into the yard, she cried, 'Mama, Mama.'

Louisa emerged from the dairy. 'My goodness, what is it, Charlotte?'

'It's fire, Mama.'

They stood at the door to the dairy as the cool, tomb-like air swept out of the room and past them.

'My God,' Louisa uttered as she raced to the clearing, where she could get a clear view. She tried to gather her thoughts. 'I must tell the family. Run back down to the lake. Make sure the oars are ready on the boat if we need it. God help us all.'

'No, Mama, please, I want to go with you. Please, Mama.' Charlotte pleaded, chilled by the word family and now a child's understanding of what that meant.

'I'll not have you defying me, child,' Louisa said forcefully. 'Go now or I will thrash you. I'll come down with the family.'

'What about Papa?'

'He's in the gully by the creek. He knows what to do. He has been through this before. He's safe there.' Louisa shut the dairy door and rushed to the homestead, scolding Charlotte when she saw her standing motionless. 'Go, child. Go.'

Charlotte remained watching her mother wildly, as a mass of cloud distended above the forest. The dog whined beside her.

'What if you can't get away from them, Mama?' she asked the disappearing form.

No reply came as the figure receded into the chaos of twisting, deformed branches and the incessant frenzy of leaves and twigs.

'I can't leave her with them,' she confessed to Paddy.

She fearfully and disobediently followed her mother and settled breathlessly close to the suicide tree. From there, she could see the homestead. Crouching, Charlotte could occasionally hear her mother raising her voice. Within minutes, the girls were being rushed to the lake track by Mrs Walsh.

Shortly, Charlotte would follow, when her mother was safe.

Charlotte crept from her hiding spot and peeped out to see Mrs Spencer hurrying to the lake track. But where was her mother? From inside the house, the slam of windows and doors shutting reverberated. It seemed an age. The dog, all sharp eyes and ears, whined and panted.

'Please hurry, Mama,' Charlotte whispered. 'Please.'

The smell of smoke surrounded them now, speeding on the searing wind.

At last, her mother appeared from the house and started to head to the track, but she stopped and doubled back.

Charlotte gasped. 'No, Mama. What do they want you to do?'

Louisa went to the chicken coop to release the birds.

Suddenly, Charlotte let out a cry. She felt something on her arm. The terror for her mother's safety had consumed her entirely and she had not registered the burning twig scalding her arm. She then noticed debris being hurled alight, all around her. The roar became thunderous, like something from the underworld.

Louisa rushed to the path.

'Mama,' Charlotte called.

But her mother did not hear her.

'Come on, Paddy,' she ordered the dog, but he stood petrified. 'Come on, you stupid dog.'

He yelped and shivered.

A flaming branch tumbled from above and onto the track near the suicide tree, cutting Charlotte off from her mother.

Louisa looked back to see the horror.

Great draughts of suffocating air swung around, nearly knocking Charlotte down. The sky flickered blazing embers amid torrents of fire-sticks spearing fire.

Charlotte tried to race, to find a way. She sucked the superheated air.

From the suicide tree to the path was an eternity. She tried to run but gained no distance. Her small legs locked into position. 'Mama, Mama,' she screamed into the wailing wind.

The dog howled.

Upon the tableau, Charlotte could see Mrs Spencer in the distance forcefully restraining Claire. The figure of her mother shimmering through the heat haze, drawing her arms toward Charlotte, running, mouth opening and closing, her face deformed and tortured.

Then blackness.

The forest blazed and brutalised and overpowered.

The suicide tree cracked violently and the chain that hung upon it was flung red-hot onto the path, embedding its definition like a branding iron, creating a scorching division between Louisa and the Spencers that required either party to bravely step beyond it.

The Visitation

Just in front of the burnt-out house was his favourite spot. Next to the gully of saltbush, mirror leaf and tea tree, hunching into a protective huddle, was the windswept knoll. From there, the toughest grasses and tussocks sprouted. It overlooked Bass Strait, the capricious beast of water that sometimes slumped into pet-like acquiescence and sometimes leapt into fits of unprovoked aggression. And sometimes offered pearls to seekers.

The hint of a northerly inflicted an irritation in him, of which the only salve was the sensation of an effervescing sea swell.

The rust-pocked car was parked with no regard for convention on the gravel cul-de-sac. Hastily vacated, it was neither angled nor straight and barely off the road. Crackling from the one working speaker, Marty Robbin's 'The Streets of Laredo' wafted out of the open window. It was the escape vehicle from the tyranny of life's afflictions, that being the microscopic views of fellow workers who made an art form of being disagreeable or the ever present river of debt that gouged a hole in his psyche.

With just the right amount of urgency, the dawn breeze teased his sun-bleached hair and hustled the flaps of his tan parka seaward. Standing on the cliff edge, legs slightly apart and arms folded, he narrowed his green eyes and studied the two points where the incoming indigo crests were pounding craggy ramparts of basalt. This part of the preparation entailed serious consideration; the sets, the breaks and the crowd were scrutinised. Any ill-conceived decision could mean hours floundering in docile waters feeling like your popsicle toes were shark bait or, worse still, being invaded by a myriad of grommets deftly pinching the ultramarine pickings. But even then you could be tricked.

Having made his decision, there was no time to lose as he gripped

the surfboard close to his side and hurried down the track that split the cascading succulents and ran to the beach. With a jump in heart rate, he raced from the sand towards the cold, bubbling shallows. But as his eyes were pinned to the waves, he failed to notice a broken shell jutting out from the sand which ripped the skin of his big toe. 'Shit,' he thought with annoyance, 'sharks can smell blood.'

The bite of ice-cold water nipped around his feet, constricting his blood vessels and stemming the bleeding. The wash crested and fell, crested and fell, the synergy exciting the senses. Wading deeper, he threw the board onto the surface of the water and jumped on. He pushed through the first wave and felt the gush flow over the board and shock exposed skin through patches on his holey wetsuit. 'New wetty, number one hundred and fifty on the list of things urgently needed and unable to be paid for,' he registered at a subconscious level.

He dived through the next few waves and paddled towards the reef break that hacked into the straight and scoured the hollows into waves. There were three others there.

'Hey,' he greeted a kid who hopefully had no idea and who he might be able to grift a wave off. 'Mate,' he nodded to a bloke who assumed pole position like a local, and a girl, further out and untouchable.

Floating on the mopey flatness, he eyed a set of waves forming. Lunging forward, he set himself in motion, positioned on the beach side of the local. He felt the pull of the sea sucking back, mounting and intensifying.

The local snatched the first wave of the set and ripped through the sun slicked water as it surged towards the beach. He paddled furiously for the next wave and had to abandon the effort as the pesky kid blitzed through and zipped onward. The next was his. Arms thrashing furiously as the momentum of the wave thrust him forward, he gripped the sides of the board before planting his feet beachward. Gradually crouching, he wrangled the shifting water in a finely tuned balancing act. But he couldn't make it stick. He lurched forward and upended. He popped up, frustrated to have crashed out, but keen for the next wave.

He set off again on a lump of water that rose and succumbed limply without breaking. The next wave was a wall. He took off too late and was hurled into the churning water. The surge pushed him down until his breath nearly ran out. He burst through the surface, gasping, and was attacked by another breaker.

'Not my day. Not my year,' he thought as he slapped the water with his hand.

The girl, the local and the kid slalomed past him again and again as he flapped about like a netted fish.

He had been so hopeful. The conditions were perfect. He had submitted to the omnipotent power of the sea to soothe and wash away the grubby, temporal grime. He had sought the great juggernauts of waves to purge him. But his skills had evaded him. Was it the extra beer last night or the long hours on the machines? His faith had been shaken. Typical.

Eventually, he was left alone as the tide slid out and offered only measly waves. Any respectable surfer was already hoeing into their fourth potato cake at the fish and chip shop and congratulating themselves on a morning well spent.

The sun pushed into the sky, signalling 'go home o'clock'. The beach crowd was plundering the rock pools and edging closer. He felt the heat on his left shoulder. Lulled by the calm, he drowsily willed the placid patch of water to offer up one last wave. One last hope. So he waited. And waited.

It was almost imperceptible. Anything can make a current in water; seaweed, schools of fish, your own stupid, injured moving toe. But not fast like that. Not a flash and then it's gone. A hurtling mass. Menacingly close. Dark. Swift. Monstrous. It makes a surfer dread.

His eyes dilated. His heart raced. His mouth gaped. He flung himself prostrate onto the board and dared his arms to enter the water and propel himself to shore. 'I'll do a Mick Fanning and punch the bastard!' he thought in a crazed flurry of reactions. His arms spun like rotary blades. The beach seemed a lifetime away as he frantically drove himself forward.

And there it was in front of him, slipping through the last-gasp, lickety little waves that slumped onto the beach. Black. Fleet. A fin cutting circles into the surface around his board. A gruesome, prehistoric killing machine.

Only it wasn't. There were no fins. There was no killing machine. There were only flippers. A whiskery nose snorted out of the water and disappeared. And then the shiny doglike face surfaced again. Its pensive eyes pierced his soul and its absurd little ear turned slightly as though it were listening.

'Hey, buddy,' he sighed to it as it dived and flicked him with a rainbow spray as though it were blessing him. And then the creature was gone, descending into the profound, shifting depths and, with it, the silvery ribbons of his thoughts.

After putting the board away and struggling to peel off the wetsuit, he sat in the driver's seat and stared ahead, becoming aware of the sun cooked heat in the car. It sizzled, cranking his spirit up a notch. He gazed at the sea to a point on the horizon where his mind seemed to be carried by the creature. From that point, if he were to emerge above the waves, another horizon would appear at a point beyond. If he were to move to that next point, another horizon would appear and another. There was no end of new horizons. If he were to look back from that point in the sea where he focused, to where he was now, the scene would appear distant, softened and insignificant.

He had come to the island in search of one thing this morning and was gifted with another. Staring through the haze of a weathered windscreen, he had to take some time to think about that.

Something Red

Wanda hotfooted it across the scorching sand as she made her way to the rocks. She barely noticed the pale young girl in red bathers who watched her closely from beneath the angled umbrella.

She placed her feet tentatively on the uneven surface of burnished basalt, heading towards the point where the waves flooded into the veins of rock like blood. The gutters gurgled. The percussive thump of hurled sea into walls of rock vibrated like a nervous heart. The air was busy with noise. It buffeted gulls and churned the water. Wind-whipped strands of raven hair flicked across Wanda's face and into her eyes. She looked up to see the frenzied birds and vigorously breathed in the sea air.

On her way to the water's edge, she saw a large rock pool and stopped. She was struck by its contents and knelt beside it. The surface of the water was relatively calm, the level being low enough to be sheltered from the wind. Around the edge she saw the limpets crunched together like clenched teeth. Tiny fish flashed quickly through the water and fled like felons when she moved.

The bottom of the pool was sandy and soft-looking. The water was so clear that she wanted to immerse her face in it. She ran her fingers over the surface, picking up droplets and causing wavelets. It was the temperature of blood – the transition from air to liquid barely noticeable.

Wanda tried to judge the depth of the pool, allowing for the deceit of foreshortening. She threw a pebble in and watched its slow descent. The water would come up to her shoulders, she guessed. She slipped a hand into the water and reached down, feeling deliciously little resistance. She scooped a handful of water out, emptying it onto the heated rock, and felt the sudden coolness of air upon her wet skin.

She decided to dangle her legs into the tepid water; the soft kiss of liquid, yielding. Glints of chrome light slit the mellow topaz as her legs shifted, feeling weightless and otherworldly. Gradually, she eased the rest of her body in; sliding into the colourlessness. Feet feeling for the sandy base. Feeling. Falling. Body sliding down, down. Neck, eyes, hair. Ears hearing echoes of her own circular movement. Urgent bubbles swiftly escaping. Beyond. Breathe. Feet feeling. Search for breath. None. Liquid flooding, eddying, possessive. Heart quickening. Eyes open. Blur. Legs kicking. Arms flailing. Fight. Hair strands ornamental upon the surface of the rock pool like damascene.

At last, her hands grasped and found the jagged edges of the rock pool. Bursting to the surface, she grabbed onto the craggy formations, cutting her arm and spilling her blood. Gulping air, she struggled to heave her body out of the suck of the water. Goosebumps reared up on her skin and the rocks burnt her. But she didn't notice. She only noticed the surface of the rock pool, the choppy surface gradually subsiding after the turbulence. In a minute, it was still again. Silently enticing. Calming beguiling. The faint ripple from a wind gliding far too low troubled the surface lightly, but the illusion of serenity prevailed.

As the sun dried the droplets from her purple skin, she faced the beach behind her, feeling as though someone were watching.

Standing up, a little shakily, she abandoned going to the point. Warily, she dodged the flooding crevices and made for the higher ground. There amongst the shale, she was safe. She climbed the cliff face to the top. She watched the water sweep across the beach as sets of waves beat in relentlessly. Sitting amongst the spikes of spinifex, she could see the distant ocean where the amplitude of blues dissolved into heaven. The seagulls soared upward in front of her, ravenous, scrounging, bot birds.

She then observed the rocky outcrop that she had previously been clambering over, and then turned her attention to the rock pool.

Wanda stood up suddenly. She sucked in air. It took a moment to understand. Upon the invisible surface of the water in the rock pool something was floating. Something motionless. Something red.

The Lighthouse

The path to the old lighthouse was treacherous at night. Some of the rocks that supported the path had tumbled into the sea or been washed away, so that it was discontinued in places. At those points, the sea would rush in and out. To continue along the path, you would have to synchronise a jump across the cavity with the receding water. If the tide was very low, you could scramble across in some places without getting wet.

The tide was coming in and Danny fearlessly bounded into darkness. Cameron hesitated. He could hear Danny's feet touch down against a surface and followed his white T-shirt with his eyes as it rose to the path.

'Jump now, ya girl,' he beckoned Cameron.

'Shut up,' Cameron snapped, trying to summons his concentration and will himself across.

'Now.'

'No. Shut up and stop bugging me.'

The sea at once flooded around the rocks, rumbling like a stomach.

'I'm going,' Danny said as he turned his back on Cameron ready to walk up the path.

'No. Wait. I'm coming now.'

Fearing he would be left, Cameron made his ill-timed leap. He could feel the damp sensation of water swishing around his feet as they touched and then slid down the seaweedy rock.

Danny laughed and called, 'Idiot,' as he heard Cameron tumble.

Cameron cried, 'Ow,' as his knee hit a sharp edge that ripped his jeans. His heart raced as he felt himself falling and could picture being thrust into the raging sea. He slipped further, becoming immersed in salty water, but as he bumped down to the depths, he realised that the water was only up to his knees.

Danny was nearly wetting himself with laughter. 'Come on, get up or evil old Salty will hear ya comin'.'

Cameron pulled himself up, grabbing and feeling the grit and pock-marks on the rough igneous rocks. He felt something like ooze and withdrew his hand immediately with disgust, and was glad Danny didn't see him do it.

Further along the path with the sea splashing along the walls and occasionally spraying them, they encountered another breach. This time, their view was aided by the light at the end of the jetty across from them. It flickered intermittently, plunging them momentarily into darkness. Again, the timing of the leap had to be just right. Danny jumped like a gazelle during a trough and landed sure-footedly on a large sloping rock. As the soles of his feet were dry, they clung on until he stepped onto more even ground.

Cameron baulked. 'I'm not comin'.'

'What?' Danny asked emphatically. Then he shrugged and said, 'Okay,' and added, 'good luck getting back.' He threw the line, wily as an angler with just the right amount of bait.

'Just wait till I climb down here,' Cameron said as he pondered being marooned on the path in the dark and alone with the risk of an encounter with old Salty.

'Hurry, there's a big one comin'.'

Cameron clambered back and watched the wave spill into empty cavities and splash up and over the rocks. As the wash abated, he stepped down and leapt. His shoes touched down on the rock and, as the soles were wet, he slid awkwardly. He grasped and held on tena-ciously, remaining upright. Danny didn't see.

From here to the lighthouse, the path was intact, although sloping in parts. Danny threw some stones into the tossing tea as he walked. Cameron followed him but turned to survey the beach and the dotted lights of the Safe Haven Caravan Park now hidden behind the tea tree.

He noticed a figure on the jetty and wondered if the person was watching them.

'Come on,' Danny said, 'let's scare the old fool,' as they neared the lighthouse.

Cameron felt the uncomfortable surge of blood burning up his cheeks and plumping up his chest. It was the same overwhelming feeling he had experienced when he had tortured himself and entered a race at the school swimming sports to test his mettle. He half drowned but staggered out of the pool exhilarated.

He watched Danny swagger. The charismatic coolness that drew Cameron to him now appeared as detachment. It was calculating, risky and cold. Cameron realised that Danny had little need for him. Suddenly he felt lonely and glanced across to the figure on the opposite pier.

As they came to the lighthouse, Danny pushed on the door. It did not yield. He bumped his body against the door. Nothing. Then he picked up a lump of driftwood from the rocks and thrust it at the door. 'Come on, help me,' he commanded Cameron.

Cameron and Danny heaved their bodies at the door, with Cameron apprehensive about what would happen if they got in. Still his heart pounded and the adrenalin raced around his body, making him feel bigger and stronger in contrast to his usual timidity.

'Let's smash that rock against it,' Cameron said with reckless excitement.

They heaved it with no luck, and then Cameron stopped for a minute, considered and said, 'I think it opens out.'

It was open. All the time, they had been forcing it back., They laughed madly.

'Yeah, I knew that,' Danny boasted.

The door creaked painfully when they entered and Cameron ducked as cobwebs fell in streaky threads.

'Scared?' Danny taunted wildly as he took to the stairway.

He climbed in the darkness. At the first landing, he took the matches out of his pocket and lit one. Cameron looked up to where Danny stood; his face distorted and grotesque as the wavering light flicked illusory expressions upon it. The whiteness of the walls reflected back in a battle with the darkness. But mainly they were engulfed by shadows.

Slowly, they ascended the stairs. Cameron was constantly feeling for the steps and rail in an effort not to stumble. He lagged behind Danny, who continually lit matches to illuminate his own way and then tossed them carelessly when they were still alight.

'Come on, you little baby,' Danny said forcefully back down to Cameron, who was stepping blindly and hearing his own pulse thumping in his ears.

He heard Danny blow out a match and stop. 'Shhh,' he whispered.

Immediately, Cameron halted. He heard his own breath thundering in and out of him and wished he could stop it. He shuddered while straining to listen. Gauging the number of steps he needed to retreat, he looked back down into the darkness. He heard a thump. It felt like a cold gush of air had hit him. Then he heard a howling scream.

He plunged back down the stairs, missing a step and landing on his bum. He quickly regained balance and jumped from the stairs onto the floor rushing out the door. He looked over his shoulders to see if Danny was following.

He raced to the first break in the path. The sea surged, sloshing and gouging. He could see the faint whiteness of the foam. The tide had risen. The gap had widened. It was too far to jump.

Danny hadn't come out. Cameron stood watching, breathless. His eyes focused on the gaping door. The waves relentlessly hissed around him, harsh and scornful. He scowled and strained his eyes. But Danny did not emerge. Time stretched like an elastic band. A niggling relic of conscience forced him back to the lighthouse. He walked slowly, allowing generously for the chance of some kind of intervention to occur. He shook. He was ready to run away. But where?

As he reached the door, he nearly lost his nerve. But a good man will always go through with an act of courage. He touched the handle as though it were explosive. Pulling it towards him, he stepped inside. Clammy darkness surrounded him.

Cameron stood listening, silent and motionless. Suddenly, he was gripped. From the blackness, fingers encircled his neck. Tentacle like they slithered, squeezing. A screeching sound engulfed his ears. He could hear himself shriek. Evil Salty – it's evil Salty, he thought with horror. Fear nearly forced his guts out.

The fingers relaxed and the screeching stopped. It was replaced with maniacal laughter – booming and aggressive laughter – Danny's.

'Gotcha, gotcha,' he mouthed as he hunched with paroxysms.

Cameron was on the brink of tears. His chest was bursting. He was grateful for the darkness.

'Come up here, ya girl. Have a look from the top,' Danny yelled to Cameron as he rushed up the stairs.

Cameron barely recovered his breath. He felt the intensity of rage and relief and sniffed, 'I thought it was Salty.'

'Salty? There is no Salty, you idiot. I can't believe you thought that story was true,' Danny said as he pounded up the steps again.

Cameron stood up. The scar on his knee and bruises were throbbing. He took the stairs with a rush. He could see Danny's legs above him and felt like striking them. He suppressed a sob and it made him feel deranged. Anger was swirling like a cyclone – it was ready to lash. Hate flashed momentarily in his psyche, making him want to push Danny down the stairs. He snatched at the rail. With his eyes now accustomed to the dark, he was not so blind any more.

Through the window at the top, the boys scanned the horizon. Cameron stood a little behind Danny, panting. His eye roamed from the caravan park, across the beach, along the pier and the figure on it, to the channel markers, but his view was interrupted by a void of light in the form of Danny's head, square and impenetrable. Cameron pinned his eyes on the back of Danny's head. He wished he had the power to slash something, to sweep it aside both physically and mentally. His eyes searched momentarily on the floor for some kind of weapon, but as Danny moved, Cameron gazed past him to the channel markers, which were blinking safe passage, guiding the ships to harbour.

A flash of light appeared as Danny lit a cigarette. He offered one to Cameron.

'No. My grandma smokes. They stink,' he said accusingly.

'Well, you should be used to it then… That's where I got 'em.'

'Where?'

'From your grandma.'

'Did she give them to you?'

'No, stupid. When she came to your cabin with your aunty the other day, I nicked them out of her bag.'

'Why?' Cameron asked, feeling his breath stick in his guts.

'Coz I wanted some smokes.'

'But they're hers,' Cameron reasoned, feeling puzzled and cheated.

'Well,, they're mine now. Besides, she shouldn't be smoking,' he offered with twisted logic. He flicked the lid shut while he drew the smoke in and screwed his face into an ugly, sadistic expression. He lit another match to get a better look around.

'You shouldn't do that up here. Someone will see. We'll get caught.'

'Who cares? Besides, I'm the light for the lighthouse,' he smirked.

'We'll get into trouble.'

'So?' He held the match out and studied the surroundings.

The top floor of the lighthouse was bare save a layer of filth that compacted at the walls and entombed moths, spiders and the grains of thwarted intent from others who had been there. The light had been taken out years ago and the spectacular prism dismantled and taken to the council yards and stored in a shed. All that remained was the shell of the building, the rotting stairs, the corpses of imprisoned birds and the spectral presence of Salty.

Names were scrawled onto the walls, and Danny pointed out to Cameron the mark he supposedly made when he had come before.

Cameron looked at it and thought he would like to scratch it out. 'That's graffiti,' was all he could say.

He felt shivery and wished that he was back in the cabin that his parents were renting. He wanted to be pyjama-clad and tucked up in his sleeping bag listening irritably to his younger sister snoring into her pink bear in the bunk below. He regretted agreeing to stay at Danny's house for the night and telling his parents that Danny was a good kid and that he had met Danny's parents. He would be forced to invent more stories tomorrow about Danny's house, Danny's folks, Danny's toys, what they had for tea, for dessert, for breakfast and how they spent their time.

He could call them stories all he liked but they would carry the weight of lies. He felt that part of him had been knocked; a chunk toppled and, like the rocks he had tumbled on, had rolled to the depths. He was unsettled by how easily the rocks had fallen and the foundations weakened. He recalled the first chink forming when he and Danny had forced their way through the gap in the wire and punched the warning sign out of the way.

The cool south-westerly had picked up and Cameron heard its distressing howl as it forced a way through the cracked windows. It sang off-key, rising to a crescendo like a warning siren. The whitecaps were just visible moving crazily down the bay. The temperature in the lighthouse was falling and Cameron hadn't foreseen how cold the night would be. The words of his mother came to him, as she would often remind him, 'You have to think ahead – think about the consequences.' The words bit into him like gnawing rats. He had never known before how long a night could last. He was unsure what time it was and his eyes were salt-rimmed and stinging. He thought about how the tide and sea would now determine his fate.

'I'm cold and tired. I'm going to see if I can get back,' Cameron announced.

'You can't. The tide won't be out yet,' Danny said confidently.

'I'm going.'

'Suit yourself. But it'll be higher. Those waves are pretty rough now,' Danny challenged.

'Whatever.'

'It's not going to be worth it. You're stupid and crazy to try,' Danny advised derisively, grappling with the rebellion.

Cameron felt the walls and the cold, rusty metal rail as he stepped deliberately on the stairs. He brushed off the mesh of spiderwebs distastefully when he reached the grimy ground floor of the lighthouse, and he could smell the stench of something rotting which he hadn't noticed before. He opened the door and was overpowered by a rush of wind. He allowed it to assist him back down the path.

Seaspray showered Cameron. He felt fleshy like a soft fruit as he hugged himself against the battering wind. He turned and noticed the lights of a tugboat, which were bouncing and jigging towards the mouth of the bay to guide a tanker. The comforting pulse of the motor drummed across the water. He looked across to the figure on the pier and felt surprised that they were still there, but relieved that he was not alone.

At the first break in the path, the tide appeared no higher, but the waves gushed in with wind-driven ferocity which made the leap even more dangerous. He stood for a few minutes and watched. He tried to judge if there was a cycle in which the waves would abate enabling him to jump. But he was too tired; the weight of fatigue irresistible. Even with the continual assault of the elements, he pressed his head into his knees and drowsed as the earth turned. From the jetty, he would have appeared like an embryo.

He awoke with a start as his head lurched forward. Unaware of how long he had drowsed, he was convinced dawn was close as a suffused aura appeared in the east. A filament of cloud blazed as though it were electrified. The sea had calmed and breeze had dropped.

Cameron stood tall and stretched. He walked to the edge of the path and watched the sea glide in and out, sending wavelets skittering across the faces of the rocks. Moving closer to the edge, he calculated the distance to the shore. He looked across to the pier and realised that the figure that had given him solace during the night was a misshapen bollard. He was alone. He breathed in deeply.

He looked back to the lighthouse, darkly dominant against glisten of pearly light. He fancied he saw the outline of Danny's face watching him from the gloom. Or was it old Salty? 'You are evil, old Salty,' Cameron said as the morning light burst upon him before he dived in.

Clouds

Imogen leant forward, grabbing the greasy rail, licking spume as the ferry plunged into the green trough. She stuck her head out from the rear of the boat and searched the horizon, glimpsing the island through squinting eyes. She recognised the two distant bumps, wart-like on the water, which appeared as two distinct islands but were in fact one. She sat back on the floor of the deck against her backpack. The outline of the port with its skeletal cranes piercing the sky and the severe outline of tenements was disappearing through the metal bars. Beyond that was the granite inselberg, Breaker Hill, that butted the sky like a prize-fighter's head. The swell swamped the exhaust fumes that spluttered out of the rear of the ferry like flatulence and a sickly trail of white wake extended behind them, washed and smashed until it merged with the black blue sea. Satisfied with the view, she took from the pocket of her spray jacket a day-old sandwich.

The ferry was mainly filled with holidaymakers. Imogen gazed at them lazily as she munched. A young girl smiled in her direction as Imogen pulled pieces of crust off and threw them overboard to the delight of the scrapping seagulls. The girl was pulled back by the mother whose bulbous sunglasses dazzled in her direction. Imogen stared at the family and imagined that if the boat were to sink they would all be equal in the eyes of saviours. The mother readjusted her glasses and held tight to her dress that dared to flare in the slipstream. The father looked as though he had been loaned out by his office, like a book from a lending library, unexposed to holiday sunlight.

Within sight of the ferry terminal, Imogen stood and edged to the exit to be the first off. She lifted the deflated backpack, which, although she laboured to pull over her shoulders, was virtually empty. She pulled her cap down over the wiry hair and surveyed the procedures to secure the boat as the ferry bumped in. People were massing behind her but that didn't stop her from spitting out an offensive piece of sandwich into the slopping sea.

On the pavement outside the terminal, she stood for some moments in the rich sunshine like a millionaire. She drank the tepid air into her lungs hugely. It was luxurious. She bathed in the glorious warmth that freedom affords. She was free of walls, of sorrowful insufferable uniforms, free of breathing someone else's air. The island bus pulled away in front of her and she stepped back from the kerb in a kind of wonderment. She had forgotten. The smell of diesel permeated the air, but it was a kind of elixir – a reminder of liberation, the evocations of a journey, of life unrestrained and uninhibited. She nearly fell to the ground thinking about it in a fit of shock – as though she had been hiccoughed from a parallel universe.

A taxi moved up to where she was standing as she raised her hand to her head in the act of steadying herself. But it didn't stop, continuing slyly, slowly to the top of the rank, right past her, preventing easy access to the fastidiously kept vehicle.

'Creep,' she called, 'you think I don't know. I don't even want a cab.'

The motor shuddered and revved for business elsewhere.

She smiled at the sun, unperturbed by a flock of lorikeets bursting from the trees as a mini-moke sped by. She stared as the colours of the riders flashed by in a kind of tie-dyed whirl, heading north. So it was to the north of the island that she headed, where houses out-shouldered one another on the clifftop and trendy bars, cafés and coffee shops slunk into the shadows of the palm trees that shooshed the lacquered bay.

Following the mellow breeze, she shuffled out of the terminal area, past the sweating lawyer's office, Shady Designs the sunglasses outlet, the brightly lit window of Angel Threads, and continued over the rise and along the path beside North South Road. She came to a junction where one sun-laden path rose above the pressing foliage and followed the ridge where sighing tourists hung over the edges of lookouts. The other path slithered below the rubber plants and became entangled in lantana and plummeted into mosquito-infested moist gullies. By following this path, Imogen was able to avoid the swing bridge over the ravine which bisected the north-south range. The bridge dipping tenuously into the whispering gully gave Imogen the heebie-jeebies.

At sunset, Imogen appeared at the most northerly and fashionable beach, joined by the motley cavalcade of interlopers who passed the ravine to toast the famed sunset. She squinted and pursed her lips as the sun hovered above the horizon before sinking and shattering a host of stars; she preferred the sun up.

Along the esplanade, people raised glasses and laughed because they had the freedom to do so. As she paused at Tex Mex restaurant, the unkempt hair, stained and faintly floral dress and mismatched plastic thongs caused second glances to fall upon her.

She eyed an empty place at the end of a table in the crowded restaurant. 'Anyone sitting here?' she asked.

'Ah no, I suppose not,' answered a woman who quickly stretched her perfectly tanned arm across and grabbed a red leather handbag which was occupying the spare seat.

'Nice bag,' Imogen said dolefully. 'I had a bag like that once. Got it from Paris. God, I loved that bag.'

Through a wineglass, the woman's eyes narrowed. 'Okaaaay,' she said as her polyester-clad bum slid along the bench seat while she raised a plucked eyebrow to her mates.

The waitress appeared and took orders for the group. She came to Imogen.

'She's not with us,' cut in polyester bum.

'Well, I can still take her order, dear,' the waitress responded.

'Of course, of course, it's just that…the bill…you know…all that stuff.'

As the meals came out, the group had squeezed together as though the table had tipped downward and away from Imogen. When the plates were dispensed, a meal was placed in front of Imogen that she hadn't ordered, but still proceeded to tuck into hungrily with grime-laden fingers.

'That old bitch has got my steak,' one of the men said, not too quietly. 'Eeeew.'

'And I've ended up with frigging nachos.'

Someone laughed at the misfortune. 'I hate nachos,' he said, a sea of irritation rippling to the surface.

The group ate and drank feverishly and then left Imogen to herself at the table.

'Still got it,' she thought as they roughly vacated their seats. Before the plates and glasses were cleared, Imogen grabbed one that was almost entirely laden with food, along with the half-eaten nachos. She poured down the dregs of a cab sav from a lipstick-stained glass. Nibbling contentedly as she watched the crowd, she summed them up as victors, vanquished, virtuous and vile.

The girl from the ferry sat pertly atop a stool with her family as they picked at their meals. She watched coolly like a seagull and her eye caught Imogen's through the throng.

The table that Imogen was occupying was gradually cleared ready for the next group of diners. Imogen hid her face as a middle-aged man stacked plates while engaging in banter with some of the regulars.

As he neared Imogen, he asked, 'You finished here?'

She raised her face and met his gaze.

'Christ, what are you doin' here?'

'Nice to see you too, Rob. I've come for what I'm owed.'

'Listen,' he said and lowered his face down to hers, 'don't come around here and start causin' trouble.'

'No, you listen, I want what's mine. For all this time, I've been turning myself inside out about what he did to me while I was rotting away in that place. I'm gonna stand up for myself. I'm gonna see your ugly, scum brother now.'

'Well, not much point – he's overseas. You'll have to come back another time.'

Imogen was struck. She hadn't planned for this. 'Where the hell is he?'

'How would I know? He goes off every year with…I dunno.'

'With her – that filthy hag. Well, thanks for nothing. You know you're so lucky. When he tried to rip you off, you had your dodgy mate to help you. Wish I was so lucky.'

'Go and see your blue healer, mate. She might fix you up.'

'Go to hell. I'm outta here. AND SHE'S A NATURAL HEALER. NOT LIKE YOU – A NATURAL HEEL!' she shouted as she got up to leave.

'Hey,' he cried as she bustled her way through the crowd, 'You need to pay for that meal.'

She pulled out two dirty fifty-dollar notes from her backpack and threw them at him, screaming, 'HERE, WAITER BOY, TAKE YOUR DAMNED MONEY.'

After tramping to the shoreline, she sat on the cool grass and watched the sun submit to the inevitable spin of the earth. Alone she sat, both resenting her life but relishing it for the freedom to stay exactly where she was for another hour.

In the stillness of the bay, the lights of the yachts reached tentatively to the beach. They blinked upon delicate ripples in cautious gestures of hope. But a swift squall saw them shrink back, chopped and cut. The outlines of the hills appeared like plundering arms, foraging for treasure in the oily water. Imogen felt the cooling sand and the grains stick to the cracks in her skin and flow like a solid sea as she walked. She stared out to the far end of the bay. The lights of those houses bounced expansively off hefty concrete partitions. One, though, sat in darkness seemingly recoiling from the light as though in shame.

Dragging her backpack along the beach, Imogen set off to the house, which stood in darkness. The road to the house had not been graded for some time and Imogen tripped over deep ruts as she climbed higher, cursing in the darkness. The noise of revelry died away until the dominating sound was that of the trees and palms flapping and the collective gasp of waves collapsing in on themselves. Resting for a moment, she gazed back down the hill and could just make out the curve of the bay, as the light drained into the horizon. The arms of the hills gripped tight, up to the very fingers of rock at the points.

A driveway abutted the road and led to the darkened house. Imogen followed it to the gates. They were padlocked. Slightly rusty, Imogen felt, as she held it in her hand. Sidling along the boundary where toppling vines cascaded down sandstone walls, she found a tree branch which rested on top of the fence and climbed up. She threw her backpack over the fence onto the mound of rotting leaves and followed, crying with pain from the jolt on her bones.

Ferns and palms flapped and flicked her face. A vine clung, as though trying to restrain her. At the front door, the grandiose doorknob bent the reflection of the moon drastically. She headed to the guest bedroom window, one that she knew had never closed properly and forced it wide. She felt for the light switch but the power had been turned off. She found a candle, which she lit and placed on a table, carelessly spilling wax. She dreamed of burning the house down, but that hadn't worked the first time, so she bedded down like a shabby moonraker.

Through the night, the weather had changed.

Imogen sat at a café and drank black coffee. 'You come here for the sun and where is it?' she asked no one in particular.

Shoulders hunched at tables beside her.

'Do you think it will last?' she asked the waiter as he brought her toast.

'It doesn't look good for the next few days. We're supposed to get rain today. We never get rain this time of year. The weather bureau said it's an upper level trough. I dunno what that is, but it doesn't sound good,' he moaned as he stared out at the beach incredulously.

Rain in the dry season unsettled the islanders. Clumps of remnant nimbostratus clouds dishevelled the hilltops. The boats bobbed as though they were on crack. Waves clashed, frothed and leapt flotsam, exposing skirts of seaweed along the edges of rocks.

Imogen kicked out at shelly mounds when she walked along the beach and pulled out her phone. 'Hi, Barb…yeah, I'm back… You okay for a visit? Yeah, good. Come to get me money…no, he's supposed to be away with that…yep…ha, oh him…yes…he called you a blue healer! What a charmer…yeah…I'll see you…dunno, an hour or two? Nah, I'll walk…no, no I want to, after all that time shut up in that place, it's good to get fresh air, I'm good with it…yes, I'll take care…I will… See you soon.'

She started to walk along the beach, but the nervous disposition of the crabs irked her. 'Everyone's pissed,' she noted as her gaze passed from the beach to the sky.

Water swirled – cleansing, sweeping, circling, reclaiming. Imogen was convinced that the clouds were following her from the south, deep; from the chthonic origins of Melbourne alley grot and soaking, weeping institutions. The drench caught in the upper trough, debauched and drunk on its own audacity, had bumbled right up the coast. The sea told her as much. She backed away from it, shinnying up the cliff face where she met the North South Road and followed it until she could cross to the inland path. Swift showers whipped past, misting the road as though it were polished, but in reality gathering exquisitely tiny grains of dirt into infuriating balls of grime.

At the first scenic lookout, she hung on to the rail and turned abruptly. Although not admitting it to herself, she was relieved to hear a family traipsing up the hill. They passed and nodded hello. The girl had dropped her drink bottle and Imogen picked it up and gave it to her.

'Hi, little girl, we meet again. Pretty dress.'

'Thanks. Mum told me not to wear this dress hiking. She said a white lace dress was a bad choice. She's got a thing about bad choices.'

Imogen handed her the bottle.

The girl stood, hesitated thoughtfully and asked. 'Was that man at the Mexican place mean to you last night?'

'Yes. And so is his brother. They're nasty. His brother owes me a lot of money and he sent me away…

The mother placed her brilliant Nikes between Imogen and the girl while flashing a guarded smile, 'Gotta go, Angela. Bye.'

Looking down upon Peaceful Bay, Imogen could hardly recognise it. The water was riven by snivelling spits of rain that washed the turquoise out of it. Scudding cloud had dragged the sun off somewhere. Suddenly, her confidence deserted her. She could feel the familiar cold vein of fear throb through her body. The beasts of resistance cowered, submitting to the gloom and descending into hibernation. She clutched the rail tighter, regretting that she had arranged to walk to her friend's house. But the heady draught of freedom had made her giddy and she thought that she could imitate a normal person. Each step away from the main road put her in a cold sweat.

She was rattled by a presence. 'Was he here? Don't be stupid, he's overseas,' she told herself. 'Idiot woman, idiot woman.' And then he was there. In her head. In the tea tree. In the wattle. In the eucalypt. In the very grey dirt. Dripping from the sky. Growing in strength. Repeating his words until it became her mantra 'idiot woman, idiot woman'.

Each step was fraught as she sought control over the flimsy thongs and wayward thoughts. If only that family would come back. She could tag along behind them. She was convinced that the steps she heard were not just echoes of her own and feared being alone with them.

Step by step, she edged closer to Barb's house. The mist clogged her pores and greased her view. She was close to the bridge that spanned the ravine. The raindrops were tropical now – pounding with engorged energy. Down her face and back and arms, rivulets surged until she was one with the earth as it turned from solid to liquid. The path was a river, torrential and covetous. She withstood the initial flow as the water swirled about her feet and the thongs flapped like loose tongues. Gushing into her ears was the sound of her name. He was there. The tension in her toes made her legs ache. Her heart raced, and now she was nearing the bridge, the source of fear and dread.

The rush of water sloshed over her feet and slewed the thongs sideways in an act of betrayal. She fell. On her side, she slid horribly. The momentum of the fall propelled her down beside the bridge and against a granite boulder that muscled in beside it. Arms flailing and head knocking against the rock, she grabbed wildly at wet fern fronds and vines, but the weight of her legs thrust her downward into the rushing stream. The torrent plunged her underwater and along until she became lodged against a partly submerged tree trunk, where she was able to pull her head above the flow.

Barely conscious, she clung to the branch and was battered by the force of the water and debris. She gasped as waves bulged and doused her face. She thought she was done for, but above the roar of water she could hear the creak of stressed timber as someone stepped onto the bridge. Her lips started to form the word help, but when she saw him, she stopped.

The grey figure shuffled across the bridge and became obscured by the deluge. The soft flushes of foam riding the water coiled out of the current and bubbled up her nose and ghosted her vision. Being wedged by the tree and resisting the incessant force exhausted her as she tried to pull herself to the side of the ravine. But her fingers were failing her, cramping and clamping onto the branch; her own body was incarcerating her.

Again the bridge creaked. Her lips formed, but instead of speaking the word help, a gush of water stifled it. Psychedelic patterns swirled past her eyes. At the centre of her vision, a white, luminous, angel-like figure flourished diaphanous lace wings and descended through the nodding, sopping ferns.

Twisted shapes decorated the curtains that had been drawn against the light in the humid bedroom. The sheets, though freshly laundered, did not have an institution smell, but a pungent Lever and Kitchen citrus scent. The pillow was smotheringly plump against her face.

She could hear murmuring and eased herself into a sitting position which made her groan and caused the springs of the bed to squeak.

'She's awake,' cried a young voice from another room.

'How are you?' asked Barbara, who appeared by the side of the bed.

'Not too good. My arse and my head hurt,' she said, rubbing her forehead and turning to see the child from the ferry and her family.

'Hi. It's my young friend. Nice to see you again.'

'Hi,' answered the child.

'What happened to your dress?'

'It got a bit wrecked when we got you out of the water.'

'What do you mean?'

'Leave her alone, Angie. She needs to rest,' suggested her mother.

'These people helped save you. You nearly drowned at the ravine Mo. Don't you remember?'

'What? Oh Christ, why is he here?' She wailed when she saw Rob appear from the other room.

'Stop, Mo. He helped too.'

'No. I don't believe you.' In a moment, she recollected the figure on the bridge. It was as though he and his brother were one.

'You were in the water at the swing bridge. This little girl saw you going under and her family got in and helped save you. Then Rob saw them and went down to help.'

'The doc is coming soon,' Rob said.

'NO, NO, NO,' Imogen cried and began scrambling to get out of bed. 'I'M NOT GOING BACK.'

'Relax, Mo, they're going to check your head – there's a bump there. You have a massive scar on it.'

'What? Where?' She felt the side of her head, realising that a bandage was tied around it.

'Are you sure, Barb? God, I don't feel good.'

'Look, you have a little nap and we'll let you know when the doctor arrives. Okay?'

'Yeah, okay, but he needs to go, I've got a bad feeling about him,' Imogen whispered to Barbara as she pulled up the sheet and gestured towards Rob.

'Don't stress. He said he's going to help you. We are going to help you…with everything.'

Imogen looked deeply into Barbara's eyes. They were darker than she remembered. 'Thanks, Barb,' she managed to say as she lowered her head onto the pillow and pretended to sleep.

The room emptied but Angela remained. 'I hope you get better soon,' she said softly as she leaned over Imogen and motioned to adjust the bandages as her mother returned to the room.

Imogen opened her eyes and winked.

'Oh, and we found your purse,' Angela said as she pressed a purple clutch into Imogen's hand.

Angela's mother came close to Imogen. 'We'll be in contact,' she whispered as she helped Angela pin the bandage. 'Take care, Imogen. We'll see you later.'

As Angela was led out of the room, she turned back and raised her hand to her ear.

Throughout the night, the room grew light and dark as the curtains swelled in the breeze, squeezing and stretching the light from the porch. Imogen strained to hear the conversation that was being held there between Barb and Rob, but she battled fatigue and delirium as the hours ground down to morning.

At first light, she was awake and squinting at the phone. Her fingers fidgeted upon the screen before she secreted the phone into her pocket.

At breakfast, a tray of poached egg, wholemeal toast, tea, water and a nest of capsules had been laid on the table next to Imogen.

'What's all this stuff? You know I hate taking pills.'

'One is for pain, one is an anti-inflammatory, the others are arnica and vitamins and something to make you relax. See, we're looking after you,' Barb assured Imogen as she wagged her finger. 'We want to get you well.'

'Yeah, you and who else?' Imogen placed some pills in her mouth and drank the water that she had been given as Barb watched. 'Can you please give me some more water?'

When Barbara left the room, Imogen spat the pills out into her hand and placed them into the other pocket.

'So what's with Rob an' you?' she asked Barbara when she returned with the water.

'Like I said.'

'Like you didn't say. What's with you two?'

'It's a small island, Imogen. You're always running into people. He got in touch with me about helping you is all. He said that you can leave it up to him. He reckons that he can get his lawyer friend to sort it all out. You might need to sign some papers or something,' Barb explained. 'You know how he's not fond of his brother. He wants to get him back after their falling out. He's on your side.'

'Why was he following me?'

'He knew you were coming here along the track and went there to find you, and tell you. Lucky he was there.'

'Yeah, super lucky, wasn't I?' she noted drily. 'He didn't seem so keen to see me or help me at his crappy food poisoning hole when I saw him.'

'Oh well, he's obviously reconsidered.'

'Really? Is it really for revenge on his brother?' Imogen asked as she studied Barb.

'Mmm. That's what he says.'

Imogen threw back the covers. 'I'm feeling better already. I'm going out.'

'You can't. You must be tired. You're not well.'

'Ha, I've had people telling me that all my life, Barb. Don't you start.'

'Where are you going?'

'I just need some fresh air. Don't you worry your pretty little socks off. I'm just going down to the pier, or am I not allowed?'

Misty rain drifted down as she made her way along the short track. When she reached the end of the pier, she emptied her pockets into the sea and watched the pills drift to the depths. She took out the phone and read a message.

A week later, Imogen woke early and was surprised to see the sun gild the wall with soft vertical lines from a gap in the curtains. The lines rumpled at the cracks and peeling paint, turning sunlight into filigree. The upper trough had finally donned its frowzy, stormy cloak and headed south. She was relieved. She felt golden and unburdened and her resistance return.

'Thank Christ the sun's out,' Imogen said to herself as the soles of her feet hit the cool tiles. She felt in the bed for the clutch purse. She looked at the purple leather cover and thought, 'It's not a design I would have chosen and yet I like it.' From within it, she drew out the phone. Tiptoeing to the back door, she carefully unlocked it and scurried to the path that took her to the pier.

Up before the sandflies and the blowflies, the gluttonous mosquitoes and the biting gnats, she planted her feet onto the sand. She swallowed up the emerging sun as though it was a flaring tonic of virtue and faith. Then perching herself at the end of the pier, legs swinging above translucent water, she made a call.

'Yes…eleven o'clock…okay… Rob said the papers have been organised… Yep…see you then, and…thanks.'

A dainty zephyr skipped across the water, up through the spaces between the timber beams of the pier, making Imogen's bare arms and legs tingle. She was as nervous as the sprat. The meeting with the lawyer later that morning was giving her the shivers.

At ten thirty, she rejected Barbara's offer of a ride to the legal office.

'You're funny. Are you sure you're OK?' Barbara said. 'Well, make sure you get there on time.'

'You too. You don't want to miss out on the fun,' Imogen teased as Barbara waved to her and returned to the house. Imogen's gaze lingered on Barb's frame as it disappeared into the shadows.

The tinkling play of waves on the shoreline calmed Imogen as she flung her shoes onto the sand and entered the shallows. It cooled and refreshed her. The water rose and fell against her legs in gentle loving beats, tugging and twirling the hem of her dress. The inevitable, resolute throb of the waves hinted at the potential for a greater force.

At twelve minutes past eleven, Imogen entered a doorway with bare feet and a dripping dress creating an air of consternation from those within.

The light from the fluorescent tube prevailed against the pervading gloom of the office and petered out at the yellowing walls. And even though the ancient air conditioner blew grimly, the heat was oppressive in the pokey office. Cain O'Brien greeted Imogen with a lingering 'Hiii' as he shook her hand with his and then proceeded to wipe it down the side of his pants. The only man dressed in a suit on the island, he strode about his office picking up folders and giving orders to Madeleine his secretary, as though he knew what he was doing.

'Have a seat, have a seat,' he instructed Imogen as he merrily joked, 'You know these two of course,' pointing to Rob and Barbara.

'Nah, never met 'em before in my life,' Imogen said so convincingly that Cain momentarily panicked.

Cain opened up the folder and presented Imogen with the documents, pushing them across the slippery desk with his soft hands. 'So, we've been able to work some magic and we should be able to access what is owed to you. We need you to just sign a few things here and date it…and here…and here…and you, Rob, would do the honours here when Imogen has signed.'

Imogen took the pen and hesitated saying, 'What about a cuppa for an old girl, Madeleine?'

'Oh. Oh, sure. Madeleine, would you mind?'

'Imogen, we can down a champers in a minute, love. Let's get this over with. Cain is a busy guy,' Barbara pleaded.

'I'm as dry as a Death Valley dam, Barb. I may not have the strength to make me mark on the sheet here.'

Cain, hyper-vigilant to keep Imogen content, took his own cup from the kitchenette and handed it to Madeleine. 'Gotta keep the customer satisfied,' he said deadpan.

'So, Caino, how long you been practising?' Imogen asked as the pitch of the whistling kettle built to a crescendo.

'Ah, about um, let's see, twenty-four years? Yes, twenty-four years.'

'Until you get it right, eh?' In response to the trio's tense silence, Imogen added, 'Joke, Joyce.'

Cain then responded with a perfunctory half smile while the others clenched their jaws tighter.

'But you haven't been on the island long. Where else have you been?'

'Ah. Let's see. I started in various towns in New South Wales, then I did a stint in Victoria.'

'Melbourne?'

'Yes, Melbourne,' he said indistinctly.

Madeleine slowly stirred the sugar and the milk and the tea as the drone of the labouring air conditioner filled the silence. She brought the mug of tea to Imogen.

'Is no one else gonna have a cuppa?'

'No, thanks.'

'Nah, thanks.'

'Nope.'

'What about a bickie?'

'For Chrissake!' Rob protested.

'Well, a girl's gotta have something with a cuppa. You in a hurry, Rob?'

'Just sign the frigging thing and we can all get outta here.'

'Geez, what's up you? And here's me thinking we're all having a nice time with Caino here.'

'You're the one who should be in a hurry. You could be rich in a day or two,' Rob pointed out.

'Ah, actually, it could take a few weeks…' Cain was quick to explain.

The milk arrowroot was a generic brand and stale. Imogen pecked at it and slurped up the tea. She picked up the Parker pen and studied it.

'It writes!' Rob said emphatically, twisting in his seat.

'Yeah, but will it write what I want it to?' Imogen said, turning to Rob. 'It might go all Harry Potter on me and start writing crazy shit.'

And she laughed, and nibbled the biscuit like a nervous rodent – eyes and ears twitchy.

The others sat on the very edges of their seats as the ring of her laughter bounced off the walls.

'Okay, Caino, that biscuit wasn't the best I've had, but it might have given me the strength to get me over the line – or on the line. Where do I sign?'

Cain O'Brien thanked them all for their time. He explained once again that things could take some time to process, but everything would be sorted.

As the party sought to leave the office, Imogen positioned herself at the doorway and stopped their exit.

Outside, a burst of sunlight shone through a gap in the shop awning, bathing three figures on the footpath in a transfigurative glow.

'Oh, look who's here, it's my dear friends who saved me from going under. Remember little Angela.' As an aside, she explained, 'We've actually got a date to go dress shopping to replace the white one that got damaged when she saved me.' She then proceeded, 'Katrine and Grant are up from Victoria, you know. They're staying just up the road from your place Caino, at the International.' Addressing Katrine and Grant, she said, 'Oh sorry, this is one Cain O'Brien.'

The group inside shuffled awkwardly as Imogen persisted.

'They love the island. Love it. Especially now that the sun is out. Except they've been hard at work and haven't had a chance to relax yet. Little Angela started it all. She overheard someone planning some financial shenanigans. She's quite the detective.'

An errant bank of cloud momentarily hid the sun, chilling the bellies of all crawling things on the island, before evaporating under the suns omnipotent, illuminating power.

Angela took Imogen's hand and led her to Angel Threads, two doors up, while the rest of the adults remained.

Imogen and Angela gazed at the shop window, but their attention was focused on the exchange taking place outside Cain O'Brien's office.

'That's too bad about you having to work,' Cain responded dutifully, 'what do you do?'

Katrine answered, 'I'm from the Fraud Squad and Grant works in cyber-security.'

The group inside the office froze and their faces turned ashen as though a grizzly storm cloud from the south had obliterated their sun.

Accidental Plot

The fairway looked clear – but it wasn't. Jake and Liam had snuck behind some tea trees and thought it would be funny to race out into the open and surprise Ginny as she struck her drive while the ball theoretically soared overhead. But the surprise was theirs. They hadn't anticipated Ginny's unorthodox swing and the resulting unplanned trajectory of the ball. Instead of the ball whizzing skyward, as drives are supposed to do, it veered erroneously with heat-seeking-missile-like precision right into Liam's nose.

The boys, Ginny, her twin Phoebe and Mum spent the next six hours in casualty at Bairnsdale hospital, no doubt making comments about 'eyes on the ball – not noses', 'getting double boogies', and Liam being a 'little green'.

Nice start to the family gathering, present to perform the illicit and solemn ritual of scattering the remains of Nanny Claudia. The blessed ashes had been sitting in a second-hand Bendigo Pottery container on top of the kitchen dresser, next to the Worcestershire sauce and a bottle of gin.

Back at the old family house, Uncle Glen snoozed luxuriously on Dad's favourite easy chair in front of the cricket on the TV, while Dad squashed up next the generously proportioned Auntie Sue and the device-addicted Callum, my cousin. With beer in hand, Dad flicked bottle tops at Uncle Glen, but he was as immovable as a sauce stain on a white shirt, after enduring a day in the sun fishing on the aptly named putt-putt boat *Miss Trevally* with Dad and the neighbour. Aptly named because not only did they miss trevally, they missed all other species of fish with their lines. Although Dad coveted the chair, it wasn't long before his head was contentedly slumped on Auntie Sue's shoulder, also napping.

From my vantage point on the rug next to Baz our border collie and the coffee table, I was able to witness Dad's indiscretion. Something told me that I should have intervened and woken Dad up, but alleviating the discomfort of adults wasn't my strong point, so I continued to stuff my face with salt and vinegar chips and keep my eye on the Melbourne Renegades' strike rate.

At around eight thirty, the inappropriate 'I Can't Get No Satisfaction' ringtone on Dad's phone sent him into a befuddled spin. It was Mum asking if anything had (a) been caught at the lake or (b) been prepared for dinner.

'Ah, no, not at…not yet,' Dad stammered as though it had been the intention of the housebound to take on the responsibility.

The casualty group were on their way home and Dad's inevitable admission that the fishing trip hadn't proved to be a 'loaves and the fishes' success story, confirmed Mum's decision to succumb to the sirenic lure of Awesome Fish and Chips.

We were all consulted about our order, including Callum, who I thought had lost the gift of speech, and Uncle Glen, who magically awoke at the mention of food. After twenty-five minutes when everyone was ready to eat the dog, there was a great kerfuffle as another phone call from Mum revealed that when she went to pay for the fish and chips, she found that she had left her purse on the kitchen bench in the panic to get Liam to the hospital. So it would be quicker if someone could zoom downtown with her card, or better still someone else's card, than her racing home in the van and back downtown which would eat up precious dining time.

As luck would have it, Liam's Ford Falcon was in the drive snookering Uncle Glen's Pajero and Liam's keys were with, of course, Liam. There was talk of asking the neighbour if he would mind giving someone a lift downtown, as he had done earlier on their fishing adventure, but Uncle Glen said, 'No, I'll go.' That meant it would be the first time that his virginal Pajero would have to negotiate off-road terrain by climbing the half-metre embankment at the back boundary and traversing the luxuriant bush on the adjoining property to the back road.

We all went out the back to witness it. Dad laughed a lot and took photos. I thought Uncle Glen was going to have a heart attack and we'd have to take him to Bairnsdale hospital too because he was going red and sweating. Eventually, he rammed the Pajero up the embankment and introduced it to its first scratch.

By the time everyone was home, we were all too tired and hungry to care about the upheaval to Liam's face, although according to dispatches, there was no permanent damage. He was not allowed to drink, surf or wrestle with Jake. So essentially he would resemble a bear with a sore head – a panda bear.

After we had finished fish and chips and Baz had cleaned the plates, Jake decided to get the playing cards out. Ginny and Phoebe were up for it. Auntie Sue was in. Callum answered that he would rather poke his own eyes out with a burnt stick. Liam hollered for painkillers and the others called it a night.

I sat on the sidelines waiting for the cheating to begin. Ginny and Phoebe usually took it in turns to win. They said that they were intuitive. We called BS on that. But this time, the novice Auntie Sue won. Numerous times. Her secret weapon had of course been me. From the comfort of the couch, where I was seemingly watching the final overs of the cricket, I was able to get a panoramic view of Jake's, Ginny's and Phoebe's cards as they slumped against the coffee table. I gave Auntie Sue hand gestures, nods or winks, and she was no blind man. It unravelled when Ginny upped the ante by changing positions, choosing to sit within illegal proximity to Auntie Sue. Everyone protested, and when an ace dropped from her windcheater pocket, we knew it was time that we should all stop watching reruns of *The Sting*.

As we awoke the next morning, we collectively adopted an air of gravity about the day's proceedings. There had been talk of dispersing Nanny Claudia's ashes somewhere near the nineteenth hole at the golf club, as she had supposedly spent a lot of time there. Phoebe suggested that the mouth of the two-metre talking skull at the mini-golf course would be a fitting receptacle, because when her hip went, that was her alternative pastime and Nanny Claudia was always up for a chat. Another suggestion was that her remains be popped into a gin and tonic tumbler and placed on the stool in front of her 'lucky' poker machine at the bowling club, but that was obviously impractical. However, as Nanny Claudia had been a keen swimmer and one-time lifesaver, the final consensus was the more decorous option – the beach.

It wasn't the best weather. But the day could not be delayed as Uncle Glen and company needed to head up the coast in the afternoon to attend some poor sod's surprise birthday party at the Merimbula RSL Club on the following day. And Mum had resigned herself to finally committing Nanny Claudia to the briny after an extended time next to the Gilbey's without her being able to partake.

There was a blustery onshore south-easterly. We donned our spray jackets and raincoats. As we started to trudge along the sandy path to the beach, we had a sense that it was probably going to be easier to revive Nanny Claudia than to get her into the actual sea. When we emerged from the path, the full force of the wind hit us and nearly knocked the hefty receptacle filled with Nanny Claudia's remains out of Mum's hands.

The beach was deserted, which I was thankful for. I had had visions of us being apprehended by the local undercover coppers, disturbingly producing some cuffs from their budgie smugglers, resulting in all of us rubbing shoulders with the underworld. Although not the same underworld as Nanny Claudia.

We formed a group close to the water's edge, including Baz who had been smuggled into the van by me, as Nanny Claudia had loved him.

Phoebe pulled out a crumpled piece of paper and began to read. 'Dear Nanny Claudia, you were a wonderful woman who is greatly missed by your family. We remember your fun sense of...'

At that point, a thumping wave swirled up and nearly engulfed us. Phoebe had to dash up a bank of sand and in doing so dropped the paper, which was blown along the beach. Phoebe and Jake gallantly took off after it, but they looked like they were running in porridge and the piece of paper was spirited away. Phoebe, teary, trudged back with Jake.

Mum consoled her. 'It's okay, Phoebs,' she said, stroking her hair as the wind tugged it away.

'No. No, it's not. I always knew she hated me,' Phoebe cried.

The others looked away with varying degrees of embarrassment. I felt like saying, 'Get a grip, Phoeb, she probably wasn't fussed about you, but do you really think that a low pressure system in the Tasman whipping up gale force winds was the work of Nanny Claudia?' However, I shut the hell up, as over the years my knack for voicing odes to the obvious had given rise to numerous physical and mental attacks from my siblings. Suffice to say, Phoebe eventually recovered from her paranoia and made some suitable contribution to the ceremony, although I failed to hear most of it, as the wind continued to buffet our group and then the rain started, causing us to cover our ears with our hoods. I noticed that Callum's hood was concealing his iPhone buds. Nice one, Cal.

It came time to liberate Nanny Claudia from her stoneware pot. Ideally at this time of year, we would have thrust the contents into the clear water as the waves gently kissed the shore beneath a benevolent sun. But this ceremony was going to be a fiasco. As expected, as soon as the cork stopper was pulled out, it unleashed a swirl of ash like a genie out of a bottle. Mum rushed towards the sea as the waves receded and emptied the contents in a frantic motion and hurtled back as a dumper slapped the sand. Although some of the heavier remains made their mark into the heaving ocean, the gusts hurled most of the contents into the air like shrapnel and we had to duck for cover. Unfortunately, Baz appeared to misunderstand the import of the gesture and proceeded to retrieve portions of Nanny Claudia that plopped onto the sand. Mum cried. Uncle Glen tried to hide a smirk. Auntie Sue looked on in shock. And Dad didn't dare say a word. The rest of us hightailed it, as it was about twelve degrees and, apart from our light shower-proof gear, we were all in our summer best.

It was decided that the appropriate way to conclude the proceedings was to sink a few at the pub. We were told that Nanny Claudia would have approved. I ended up sitting next to Callum, who still had his earphones in. Auntie Sue frowned them out of his ears and he started to talk to me. '

I hate frickin' funerals an' shit, you know. It's like, I just don't wanna be here. An' today was like, get me outta here. What about when that dog got a massive piece of Nanny Claudia? You know, I thought I would piss myself.'

I couldn't tell if he was sad or mad or bad. I asked him what he had been listening to on his iphone.

'I was listening to some of my music. I made it up. You know, especially for Nanny Claudia.'

I looked at him quizzically.

'You wanna listen?' He gently pressed the buds into my ears.

I was expecting deathcore or rap or emo, but it wasn't. It was electronic, a little magical and enthralling, as if a zephyr had fluttered suspended shards of ice and sent them tinkling with arctic crispness. He asked me what I thought of it. I said it was good and we were both comfortable with that, anything else would have caused embarrassment.

In the afternoon, we saw off Uncle Glen, Auntie Sue and Callum. I gave Callum a little wave, as I thought that we had made a connection. But he was looking straight ahead, thank heavens. Dad warned Uncle Glen about going too far off road. Uncle Glen smiled good-naturedly, but I think his blood pressure went up slightly.

It was a bit of an anticlimax after they had gone. Everyone was quiet for a change. I went out to the backyard and threw the ball for Baz. After a while, Baz tired and sat reverently under the wattle beside what looked like a gritty-looking pebble.

Later that night, Jake, Liam, Ginny and Phoebe took themselves off to barefoot bowls. Dad regained his throne and celebrated by cracking a tinny and hot-fingering the remote, bouncing between the cricket, tennis and races.

I caught Mum in the kitchen on her own, looking at some old photos of Nanny Claudia on the wall. 'She loved it here,' she said sadly.

I couldn't comfort her by saying that the day had gone well and that Nanny Claudia would have been thrilled with outcome, as people do in these situations, because it was rubbish; a triple disaster with the lot. So I clumsily offered, 'She'll be happy now, away from the Worcestershire sauce.'

Mum burst out crying. At first, I thought that my hokey words had caused the onslaught of tears and was mortified, but she howled, 'It was horrible. I knew it would be a disaster after yesterday. I wanted today to be…a nice send-off. And the bloody weather and Glen laughing… and Phoebe…and the dog…and Callum couldn't even…' all this interspersed with trumpeting nose blows and flooding tears. 'I'll never forgive myself…and we waited so long to do this…but we couldn't wait another damned day or two until it was nice because of bloody Glen… and everybody just raced off.'

I ventured, 'I think everyone was cold, Mum, and I don't think Uncle Glen meant anything by it, an' Callum had made some music especially for Nanny Claudia,' and I dared to say it, 'I think Nanny Claudia would have thought what happened today was funny.'

She howled again. I wished I had shut my mouth. Her tears were worse than someone giving me a whack.

And then she made some weird face. A kind of cry but her lips were turned up and she convulsed and started to laugh too. And we both laughed. And tears streamed down her face. I took her hand and lead her out to the backyard and turned the porch light on. I escorted her to the wattle tree and pointed out the pebble.

There in the half-light we dug a hole with our hands. Baz sat with his head on his paws regarding us with dignified obeisance. We held hands, said some kind words and a prayer, lowered the pebble into the tiny grave, refilled it and placed some wattle on top.

Headlights appeared up the driveway and the newly initiated bowlers emptied out of the car and surrounded us. Dad came out to see what was going on. We huddled together in the twinkling twilight gazing on the newly created memorial.

Then Baz leapt forward, stealing the wattle, and raced into the darkness. Nanny Claudia would have laughed.

Freya

The world seemed to quake as she opened the gate. I watched from behind the musty curtains of the upstairs window. The ivy arch sprinkled raindrops upon her mousy hair like grapeshot as she unhooked the rusty catch. She looked up, but I don't think she saw me. Brushing drops from her ugly army disposal jacket she walked up the mossy brick path. Thorns from the drooping rose bushes snagged the flouncing fabric of her khaki skirt.

The heavy wool of her top and the gabardine shifted about her body in an awkward battle beneath the jacket. Her tan boots were scuffed as though she danced a lot. Or kicked. One end of her maroon crocheted scarf dangled to the ground and made her look unbalanced. Maybe she was. My Ben had offered her a bed while she was here to attend the nearby hospital. He asked me not to ask too many questions about it. So what could it mean? She was an old friend of his from the peninsula. I suppose he felt obliged to help her. He was always putting himself out for hangers-on and crazies.

I could hear her knocking on the front door as the cracked leadlight rattled. I strained to lean my head against the grimy window to glimpse the top of her head as she stood waiting for someone to answer. I felt its cold resistance. I struggled to see her head and pressed my hands against the glass plate. I glimpsed the frosted microclimate that formed around the soft flesh of my hands and pulled back from the window as the outline of me disappeared.

I was angry that she was staying here in this tiny terrace house which was hardly big enough for Ben and me, let alone someone else. And we would have to be careful. Poor sweet Ben was always looking out for people. I must be on my guard for him. The next couple of weeks would be hard for us and could complicate our relationship. We were also both under pressure to finish assignments for uni. As I listened to the battering, I found myself unconsciously scrape a great chip of varnish off the pine dressing table that stood next to the window. A splinter had pierced the skin and it hurt.

Ben had answered the knocking. I could hear distinct voices of greeting for a moment. Then a door shut, enclosing the voices in a room downstairs, creating a barrier that rendered only soprano and bass notes pitching and tossing through the passage and splashing up the stairs. I leaned my head against the wall and noticed the smoke stained wallpaper curling off the walls like it ached.

The sound of a door handle opening was chilling.

Ben must have been at the foot of the stairs. 'Freya, come down and meet Annie.'

'I can't. I'm right in the middle of this essay. There's stuff everywhere. I'll catch her later,' I said, shifting papers audibly.

I could hear the creaking stairs bearing his weight.

He knocked at my door and peered in. 'Come and meet Annie, she's okay. You'll like her.'

'Later. I'm busy.'

'No, you're not, Freya. Come on now and meet her.' He drew out his hand to take mine.

I wanted to wail. The greyness of the passage to the stairs swallowed our forms so that we could have been ghosts. The eternally gritty walls by the staircase swirled past and wisps of yesterday were already evaporating as I descended.

'Hi, Freya,' she said abruptly as I entered the stuffy room. 'I'm Annie. Thanks for letting me stay. I won't get in the way. I'll be helpful.'

I felt like saying, you can be helpful by pissing off, but I didn't. I'm sure that I didn't. We were locked into the room by small talk. Each sentence belted us in tighter. I obediently avoided the reason for her being here – to visit the hospital.

Ben sat uncomfortably on the footrest, tugging the conversation out. He left the room to make coffee for us. Suddenly, everything in the room sharpened into focus. I could see the burning reflection of the fire in her eyes, and the redness of her nails.

'How long have you been living here?' her mouth asked.

'Ages, Ben and I have been here a long time. A long time,' I said evasively, wanting to let the answer float on the layers of heat in the room. I didn't want any conversation with just her. I could detect the metal in her voice and the ability of it to cut me.

Ben served coffee on the hardwood table, moving essay notes and textbooks to the very edge. Our tongues stung with cheap bitter coffee.

Annie, sitting closest to the fire, wiped the sweat above her lip. 'This room's very warm,' she said.

'Yeah, but the rest of the house is like ice,' I warned.

'It's not real flash, there's no heating in the rest of the house. We only have radiators,' Ben said safely.

The fire popped. A shower of sparks fell like incendiary devices. We all watched and very nearly drowsed. I could hear her faintly whispering.

Her dangerous nails reached across to me. 'Let's go out for dinner. My shout.'

'I can't. I've got to finish my essay, and Ben's had a hard week – he's really tired,' I answered loudly.

The violence of night, the slap of chill winds against a fair head like Ben's, the crazy voices that she could fill his head with in the maelstrom outside alarmed me.

'Won't be late. Promise.'

Ben was silent. A freaking sphinx when I needed help to counter her. I could feel him drifting away.

'Where do you normally go?' she addressed Ben.

'Just the pasta place up the road. It's cheap…and good,' he said almost apologetically.

'And where do you go, Freya?' she asked by way of separating us.

'The same place of course.'

The blood rushed to her face as she dared us. 'Let's go somewhere different. Somewhere really nice.'

I almost yelled, 'No.'

She flashed her teeth and laughed. 'I won't take no for an answer, Miss Freya.' She stood up defiantly, picked up her bag and left the room, leaving the door open to allow the frigid air to flood in.

'In here, Ben?' she called from outside his room.

'No,' I cried again, looking to Ben for confirmation. 'Isn't she staying in here?'

'No, Freya,' he smiled, 'she'd fry in here. I've got plenty of room.'

The restaurant was like a hospital: white walls, white chairs, white on the tables. The waiters patrolled us like orderlies – seizing upon us after every false move. I couldn't think straight. We sat at a table by the window. But all we could see were passing figures, hugging themselves against the dark and chill.

She called for wine. 'Love a good red, Freya, what about you?' she asked aggressively. 'I know a good one, here,' she said, pointing with those nails. Her lips crimsonly mouthed, 'Merlot, thanks. You know, it's a little winery near where we used to live. Remember this one, Ben?' she asked him as her pupils dilated and her body leaned precariously toward his.

Ben nodded agreeably, but he was just indulging her. It was just a story. I was sure the wine was from South Australia.

The clinking of china and crockery reverberated, making it hard for me to hear them.

Ben and Annie recalled stories from their hometown. People and things they knew bound them. Barely audible, they were, but inch by inch they were building walls with their words and watching me through their constructions.

'What are we having?' I urged, trying to find a crack, thrusting the menu in front of Ben.

'Hungry, Freya?' she laughed, with her teeth catching the light. 'Okay, let's eat.'

The meals arrived fiercely steaming and urgently placed. We took up the silver forks and knives, spearing reflected light at one another.

Then from her citadel she hurled words at me. 'How's yours, Freya? It looks delicious. What is it under all that sauce? Chicken?'

She knew it was, so I didn't answer.

'What course at uni are you doing?' she asked before placing the dripping vermilion pasta into her mouth.

'The same as Ben.'

'And that is…?' she asked, then directed her gaze to Ben and apologised in a surprised tone. 'Sorry, Ben, are you still studying?' Her hand touched his and she dipped her head so low that I could almost see inside it. She tossed her head, mocking, knowing. Her eyes narrowed and her mouth opened wide in the act of devouring.

'No. Not now.' Ben studied his plate and then looked up at her, and then at me.

'Oh. Okay – I getcha.' She placed the glass on the serviette in a deliberate manner, staining it with a drop of wine. She turned completely towards me and smiled with her full mouth stretched. 'Freya,' she enunciated slowly, and her bloated buoyancy was replaced with artificial gravity.

She leaned so close to me that I was overwhelmed by the heavy scent she wore. Giddy from the pungency, I felt for the edges of the table as she dug her fingernails into the air, and heard her from afar as though I were being anaesthetised. Her voice was muffled, as it had been when she had entered our house and spoken with Ben from behind the scuffed hardwood door.

'Freya, dear, Ben and I…we were thinking…that maybe you should come to the hospital…with…me…'

The last thing I remember was the glint of her fingernails. They were plunging into me and her fingers, up to the knuckles, were red.

It sounded like a restaurant – the clanking of dishes and cutlery echoing against the white walls – when the meals were delivered. But it wasn't. There was a woman in a bed next to mine who was sniffing and coughing and mumbling. There was another female across from me. She was gorging on a meal as though she hadn't seen food for weeks. It was disgusting.

I rested my head back on the pillow, shut my eyes and breathed deeply. I exhaled and my shoulders fell forward. It seemed like a sticky balm had been applied to soften my muscles and lungs but had turned foetid and yellow. My legs, arms and head felt disjointed – as though they had been separated and then glued back together, ill-fitting, constrictive, awkward and grotesque – like a puppet in a show. I was being pulled, tied and strung to conventions and expectations that catapulted me into bleak, imagineless nothingness. I spoke with someone else's voice – squeaking in registers too high and whimpering quavers. My own voice was squashed into a place deep in my guts out of reach of my breath.

I could see the cracks in everything – the walls, the water jug, the false smiles. It was blinding, as though interrogation lights were splitting through the tears and shattering everything in sight, including me. I needed refuge and rolled over to sleep and smother the glare, but as I turned, I noticed two figures blocking the exit, larger than I remembered them at the restaurant.

She was in her white uniform. I think she said, 'Hi, Freya,' but I needed to close my eyes. Ben was next to her, writing vicious notes.

Duncan Trevaniel

I will never forget the night that I met Duncan Trevaniel. My brother Adam and I had been playing a game on our computers and as Adam was about to 'kill' me, I had stopped playing in order to investigate a noise that had come from my room.

Adam was annoyed that I had abandoned the game and cursed me as I entered the bedroom to search for the source of the noise. Finding nothing out of order, I assumed that it had been a branch from the bastard jarrah that towered above the house thumping onto the roof. I stayed in my room for a while longer because now Adam was in a foul mood and I didn't want to confront that. I peered through the window at the flickering lights pinpricking Bethany Island as it rose above the slick of black sea and tangle of bush that bordered our yard.

I then noticed a figure on the dirt track that ran next to our house from the beach to the road. They wore a hoodie; odd for such a warm night. The moonlight forked off their cheekbones as they walked back from the beach. Stopping suddenly at our gate, they turned as if they had sniffed something out and then entered our yard.

A moment later, they were knocking at our door. I felt a sense of panic because our parents had gone shopping and we were told that we were not to have visitors when they were out. Dad could get really angry about stuff like that. But because my dense brother had decided to allow some cool air into the house, he had left the front door wide open with just the flimsy wire door to bear the brunt of strangers.

Making sure the lock was snibbed, I switched on the porch light and greeted the figure, who seemed to shrink back into his hoodie.

'Hi, what do you want?'

As he emerged from the shadows, it struck me that he could have been mistaken for my brother. He was the same height and had similar sharp features, but his eyes were darker and bloodshot. Maybe he had been swimming. Or maybe he was a crackhead. Or maybe he just had red eyes. His face was drawn and his scrawny arms were like sticks of driftwood.

'Is Adam home?'

I assumed that he meant Adam my brother, not Adam my father and answered yes.

'Can I see him?' he asked.

I bellowed to Adam and was relieved that he would have to deal with the heat of my dad's verbal flames making him sweat blood for receiving a visitor when told not to.

I returned to my room and stared out to Bethany Island again. It was a pastime of mine to imagine that the lights flared upon illicit activities that the people of the island operated, such as smuggling contraband or conveying illegal immigrants. Believing this, believing anything, was better than accepting that the glinting street lights traced rigid grids of domestic tedium.

After a while, I flopped onto my bed, turned on the laptop and searched up smuggling. I decided that smuggling would have been way cooler in the old days when you could run barrels of brandy up the beach and make a tidy profit.

As I considered a suitable local landing point for contraband near our beach, a voice asked what I was looking at. It was the stranger. He had entered my bedroom and was studying everything in it.

'What the hell?' I stammered.

'What are you looking at on that thing?' he inquired.

'Nothing.' I slammed the laptop shut.

'Do you play cricket?' he asked, seizing my bat from the corner of the room. He practised a forward defensive shot.

As he lifted his arms, I noticed that his clothes billowed like they belonged to an older brother, and his jeans looked like something my dad used to wear.

'Yeah.'

'Who with?'

'Just the local team, Cannonbrook.'

'Ah, the Brookers. You any good?'

'I bowl okay and make a few runs. I made thirty on Saturday. Got out LB again. Absolute crap.'

'Yeah. Idiots always say LB when it's not. Especially if one of the dads is umpiring,' he said, indicating inverted commas with his thin fingers.

'Tell me about it. Do you play?'

'Used to. Not any more.' His voice was distant, like one of those storm-beaten buoy bells tolling on a lonely rolling sea. He picked up the cricket ball and tossed it from one hand to the other.

'Were you any good?'

'You don't realise how much you and I are alike. I always got LBs. You can't trust fathers. I was only good at swimming.'

'Was good at? Don't you swim any more?'

'Long story.' He smiled and quickly lobbed the ball in my direction. 'Good reflexes.'

With that, he walked to the bedroom door, said, 'See ya soon, champ. I got people to go and places to see.'

'Wait, what's your name?'

'Duncan. Duncan Trevaniel. And you're Dean, right?'

'Yeah, that's right.'

'See ya 'round, Dean,' he said with a provocative look.

I heard him pull the front door closed and click the wire door shut. I raced to the window to see which way he would turn at the path, but he must have already gone.

His visit unnerved me. He was the weirdest kid I had ever met. I was about to ask Adam about him when my parents returned and entered the house. I heard them asking Adam if anyone had called when they had been away.

He answered, 'Nuh,' and quickly followed up with, 'Didja get any food? I'm starving.'

Then I heard some quiet discussion and Adam slam his bedroom door shut.

I stayed in my room. I felt smug. They must have found out about Duncan Trevaniel's visit and sent Adam to his room. I had expected more fireworks from Dad than just that, though.

As I was returning my cricket bat to the corner of the room, Dad entered and made some comment like, 'It's bad news.'

I thought he must have assumed that I had been thinking about my last innings. I thought it was odd, as I hadn't told him about the dodgy decision. Then he sat down on my bed. I thought I was in for a tongue lashing and that Adam had implicated me in the visitor scandal.

My dad had a grave look on his face. 'Dean, it's bad news.' He dropped his head.

I panicked and said, 'It was Adam's fault. He left the door wide open.'

Dad looked up with a curious look on his face. 'Dean, what the hell are you talking about?'

I gaped like a beached mullet.

'Dean, shut up. Uncle Robbie is dead.'

The night before Uncle Robbie's funeral, I was watching the lights of Bethany Island and imagining the usual stuff, but my thoughts kept returning to Uncle Robbie. He had been unwell for years. We called him Uncle Robbie, but he was really Dad's uncle. He had lived in an old weatherboard house a few streets away years ago, but had moved to the city when he got sick. Adam and I used to visit him at the creaking house when we were younger and sneak into the forlorn and forgotten rooms and play 'ghost' hide and seek, where one of us would pretend to be a ghost and try to haunt the one who was in hiding.

As I was staring out of the window, I saw a slight figure moving up the track. It was Duncan Trevaniel. He paused and saw me looking at him. He beckoned me to come out. It was just after eleven thirty and I had already been told 'lights out' twice, but he seemed insistent and

I didn't want him to cause trouble with my dad, so I quietly opened the front door and hurried down the path.

'What do you want? It's late, I shouldn't be out here.'

'I know, but I've got something I need to show you,' he said as he started up the path towards the beach.

'Wait, I can't go. I should be in my room, asleep. My dad will kill me if I'm not there.'

'Don't stress, come on.'

He disappeared up the path and I thought about going back home, but I was afraid that he would come back and torment me. There was something disturbing about him.

Popping his head out from behind a twisted banksia, he waved me on and then vanished again. I hurried to the spot, but he was ahead of me on the beach. I traipsed through the sand as he started to climb into the dunes.

Again, I thought about returning to my house as I laboured through the sand and along another track.

I found him crouched by the wire fence that belonged to one of our neighbours, the Mainwairings. I fronted him. I was becoming angry and told him so.

'You owe me,' he said and flashed a menacing smile.

'What do you mean, I owe you?'

'I saw your parents come in the other night. I told them that I'd knocked at your door and no one had answered. Do you want me to tell them that you let me in?'

It unsettled me. Adam must have told him about our visitor rule.

'No,' I answered, 'don't make trouble. My dad's uncle has just died and he doesn't need any more grief, plus my dad can really go off.'

'Oh, I know that,' he said with emphasis. Then he asked seriously, 'What uncle died?' He placed his face so close to mine, like Adam does when he is trying to intimidate me.

'His name was Uncle Robbie.'

'I knew him.'

'How did you know him? He hasn't lived here for years.'

'I used to visit him at the old house,' he said.

It was a lie of course. I tried to study his face as rags of cloud unravelled across the moon and cast shadows onto it. I felt the need to leave urgently and got up to go.

'Come here.'

'No, I'm going home.'

'I can see your bike.'

'My bike?' I asked shocked.

'Yeah. Over there.'

He pointed to the Mainwairings' entertainment area near their pool, where an outdoor light blazed.

Straining my eyes, I could see a Mongoose leaning against a substantial barbecue. I knew it was mine because I had painted only the top tube yellow to make it look different to my brother's. I became more angry.

Duncan watched me quietly and then casually said, 'Well?'

I turned to him with my eyes afire. 'Well, what?' I snapped.

'Well, aren't you going to get it?'

'Get it? How can I just get it?'

'You can get over the fence just there behind that bush and bring it back to the same spot and pass it to me.'

'Pass it to you?'

'Yes. The tricky bit will be taking it from where it is. But I'm sure they'll go to bed soon and you can sneak in and get it when the lights go out.'

It would never have occurred to me to just go and get it. I probably would have got my dad to ask them about it, or go to their door and ask if they had my bike. But I wouldn't have thought to just go on to their property and take it straight back. What if it wasn't mine? But that yellow painted bar was unique.

'They can't just take your bike like that. Look, they're so rich with their fancy pool and big double-storey house and everything. Who do they think they are to steal your bike?'

He was right. We knew them. They were snobs; thought they were better than us. They had everything. How dare they? I saw red and decided to get my bike back when it was dark.

Duncan Trevaniel was not at the fence when I returned.

I whispered loudly, 'Duncan, Duncan.'

I could not see him, but maybe he was watching me as I struggled to lift the bike over the barbed wire while trying to avoid getting it damaged and in doing so, ripped my shirt and skin.

When I finally landed on the other side of the fence with a thud, a light went on in an upstairs room. I froze. A face appeared at the window. I hid behind some bushes and there I remained still. The face, hazy behind the sheer curtain, looked almost like Duncan's. But my mind could have been playing tricks on me. I shivered.

Uncle Robbie's funeral was at eleven thirty. We were going to be holding the wake at our house, as his service was going to be in Cannonbrook and he was going to be buried in the local cemetery. But we had a house full of relations turn up before the service as well. Adam was out the back with some of my cousins being a smart-arse when something caught his eye.

It was my bike, of course, slumped against the back of the shed where I had left it last night so that I wouldn't make a noise opening the creaky door.

'I can't believe it,' he said, inspecting it closely. And then he called for me, 'Dean.'

I didn't answer straight away because he was always one for pulling tricks.

Then he roared, 'DEAN, YOU FAGGOT.'

The cousins laughed.

'WHAT?' I stormed.

'Look at this.'

'What? My bike? Woohoo. Big deal.'

'Well, what's this then?' he asked as he opened the shed door to reveal a Mongoose with a painted yellow top bar neatly stacked where our bikes were stored.

He could see the look of horror on my face as I witnessed two bikes that looked exactly the same. I could feel the blood rush to my face and my breath quicken. What had I done?

Dad called for us to come in and get ready. We were bustled inside and prepared for our departure to the funeral.

We were packed into the car and as we turned onto the main road from our lane I was horrified to see Tolbert Mainwairing walking purposefully down the road towards our house. His eyes seemed to drill into mine until I my head felt like it had boreholes in it. I was grateful that we were not at home.

After the church service, we arrived at the cemetery. It was familiar terrain for Adam and me, as we used to sneak in here and smoke rollies with a couple of kids from school until Dad found out and gave us a lesson about smoking that we wouldn't forget.

As we entered the cemetery, we passed Tadhg McTavish's grave. The broken wing on the angel that sat on the top of his headstone always troubled me and the inscription on May Prendergast's stone that said, 'Until the day break, and the shadows flee away' was a riddle. The grave near where we used to light up belonged to Dolores 'Lola' Harris. The plot where her sad neglected bones rested was always spiked with dandelions, and that made her alive to us as well her early death at sixteen years. Adam used to always say that Bern Crispin should have been cremated and that Angelo Marcello's angel was an ugly bitch. Adam was always reckless and irreverent like Dad. I could never say anything like that or I would feel like their ghosts would haunt me.

As we caught up to Dad and our Uncle Gary, I heard them discussing the priest's homily.

'What the hell was all that crap about the sins of the father will be visited upon the sons? He didn't even have any sons, the stupid old git.' Dad's voice seemed to ping off the monuments and rocket into the ears of the priest who was waiting by the grave.

He glared in our direction, bearing the heat of the sun as it beat back the shade. Everyone else was shuffling through dead gum leaves, reverently, like people should carry themselves in cemeteries. Even when I used to come here and smoke, I never raised my voice.

The priest said some prayers. I started to daydream and imagine hiding places where I could store a cache of arms or contraband from smugglers for the people of Bethany Island when I was jolted back to reality and asked to toss dirt on the shiny coffin. Mum cried a little but Dad was having none of it. He stood in the shade fidgeting, his fingers restless to hold a tinny.

We retraced our steps along the gravel path after the burial, except we didn't go out the main gate with the others. Adam and I followed Dad and Uncle Gary, who took a shortcut through rows of graves to get to the cars.

Uncle Gary pointed out a grave that I hadn't ever noticed before. 'Hey, remember this kid, Ads?'

'Oh, yeah. Weirdo.'

'You used to bully the shit out of him.'

'Yeah, well, he deserved it. He used to bug me.'

'What did he ever do to bug you?'

'He just did.'

'What? You didn't believe that story about his mum and our old man, did you? You were a crazy prick sometimes.'

'Sometimes?' Dad said and grinned coolly.

'Poor kid, I couldn't believe it when he went, being such a good swimmer. I remember you made him pinch that bike.'

Dad stopped, turned sharply to Adam and then to me before continuing, flashing a smile with a hint of cruelty.

I was stung. My heart fluttered. I could feel my face get hot. Was this some practical joke that they were all in on? Was Dad setting me up?

My head was thumping. My father could spin a psychological web like a lethal spider and watch as you became more entangled trying to get out. In the end, you would have to submit to your inevitable demise.

I tried to recover. I dropped back behind Adam and watched them as they continued to stomp through and trample the graves.

I took a minute to steady myself, to breathe deeply and calm down. I was sure, one way or another, that I would be in for it when the last visitor had left our house and the day was done.

For a moment, the idea of swimming out to sea and never coming back struck me. But I remained in that spot and filled my lungs with a shot of punchy eucalyptus air that swept past me from an ancient gum. I looked up at the soaring tree and noticed how its main branch pierced the sky and cut it in two; like one half was heaven and the other half was hell.

As I stared up, I became giddy and placed my hand on the head-stone for support. It took a while to get my balance. When I did, my eyes rested on the words. I sensed that someone was behind me creating a dark outline across the engraving which read

In God's Loving Care
Always In Our Hearts
Died by Drowning Aged 16
Duncan Henry Trevaniel

Leagues

She was nursing a broken heart. Having been dumped for the gazillionth time, Ziggy was too distraught to socialise with a gaggle of her cashier mates by the pier. She dropped her Hello Kitty backpack onto the sand and flung her fuchsia beach towel down.

This part of the beach was safe from her crowd. It was where the grammar school girls came sporting their boutique bathers and fake tans. She noticed a pair of them sunbaking directly behind the male and female lifeguards. They watched her as she untied her halter-neck dress and wriggled out of it to reveal an outstanding body clad in the merest crocheted bikini. Something about the way she flicked back her pink hair, exposing an arm adorned with a profusion of tattooed butterflies, made them smirk. They could smirk all they wanted. Her hair, which screamed 'take that', and her bearing announced a disarming straightforwardness.

She plopped down onto the towel, donned her scratched sunglasses and looked around. Her gaze rested on the male lifeguard. He turned and caught her watching, so she quickly turned her attention to some youngsters running to the water. The lifeguard wasn't bad. Ticked all the boxes on the ideal man sheet: good physique with well-defined muscles, and a good face with high cheekbones, strong jawline, pretty eyes and sensuous mouth without being too gross. She noted the cunning in the grammar school girls' decision to plant themselves right behind him. And although she was devastated by her recent rejection of love, the act of daydreaming eased her pain. I wish, she thought, but conceded that he was probably attached, gay or enamoured of the grammar school types.

After some time trying to concentrate on reading the second-hand Penguin, she got up and brushed the sand from where a crease had formed across her waist and oozed a line of sweat. Her body hot, she was ready for a swim.

The grammar school girls were already in, splashing around, but not endangering one another's deadly straight honey locks, presumably styled to look natural at Renee's on the High Street. Their well-aimed laughter ricocheted across the surface of the water. But the male lifeguard was in deep conversation with his colleague. A prolonged squeal was produced to gain his attention momentarily before he assured himself that there was no emergency, other than a breach of their entitlement to be the centre of attention.

Ziggy watched their game before diving in and swimming underwater for metres. She popped out of the water near an older lady whose white hair was equally prohibited from touching the water. From Ziggy's reckoning, after looking into her eyes, she guessed that the lady was probably in her late sixties or early seventies. However, the smooth skin that had been pinned back behind her ears and the boldly rounded lips gave her the appearance of few sixty- to seventy-year-olds that Ziggy knew. But the lady was pleasant and complimented Ziggy's hair colour.

'I'd like to do that to my hair, it's a statement, but my friends would probably think it was a bit wild for me,' she laughed.

Ziggy thought for a second. It hadn't occurred to her that her hair was a statement. But she assured the lady, 'You should do what you want. It shouldn't matter what your friends think, they shouldn't judge you. If they do, you might need to change to some bright-haired friends.'

Confronted with that truth, the lady smiled. 'Yes, you're right, dear. What colours did your salon have?'

'Oh, I did this myself. I got the dye from a supermarket.'

'Oh, I don't think I could do it myself. I'll have to see whether they have those colours at my hairdresser.'

'Nah, you can do it. If I can do it, anyone can,' she assured the woman before saying, 'See ya,' and swimming on.

Ziggy had drifted a fair way from where her belongings had been placed. And the lifeguard. She started to freestyle back but slowed down to allow the lady who she had been talking to slowly breaststroke in front of her.

Ziggy tipped her head back and floated for a moment, feeling the familiar sting and itch of drying salt water on her skin. She stood in the water and saw that the grammar school girls were still trying to gain the attention of the lifeguard. The lady had stopped near them and chatted to them momentarily before starting to wade to the shore.

Ziggy's eyes followed the lady. Something didn't seem right. The lady lurched to the left before she righted herself. She ploughed onward through the water and stopped to steady herself. Ziggy plunged into the sea and swam towards her. The grammar school girls remained stationary, staring and then looking the other way. The lifeguards were busy patching up a little boy who had injured himself and hadn't noticed the woman.

As she plodded to the shoreline, the woman stumbled and knelt in the shallows. Ziggy raced to her. She put her hand around the lady's waist and encouraged her forward to the dry sand.

'Oh, thanks, dear,' she said as she tried to regain balance.

With Ziggy's help, she got up and took a couple of steps forward, leaning heavily on the lightly framed Ziggy, who used all her strength to right the lady.

At this point, the male lifesaver hurried to the two of them, leaving his colleague to finish with the boy. 'Are you okay, madam? What seems to be wrong?'

'Oh, silly me. It's all right. I'm fine really. I'm just getting used to some new blood pressure tablets. Just making my head spin a bit. And getting out of the water after a swim. You know how it spins your head a bit. Thank you. Thank you.'

The lifeguard and Ziggy sat with the woman for several minutes. He brought her some water and she slowly got to her feet before thanking them both again and returning to her belongings with Ziggy following her.

'You sure you're all right?' Ziggy inquired as the woman picked up her towel and placed it around her shoulders.

'I am, you dear, sweet girl. I was lucky to have you and Mr Hand-some look after me. If it had happened on the street, people probably would have stepped over me,' she said laughing. 'You should have a chat to our good-looking lifeguard and see if he's unattached, dear,' the woman suggested to Ziggy.

'The lifeguard?' Ziggy said doubtfully. 'He's way outta my league.'

'Mmm, he looked interested to me. Two helpful people. You would suit one another.' The lady picked up her bag and turned to Ziggy. 'You know what? I'm going blue.'

Ziggy's eyes widened with alarm.

'My hair,' she said, smiling and pointing to her head.

A while later, as Ziggy dozed and sun-baked, she sensed a cool shadow being cast on her supine form.

'Hey, thanks for your help before,' the lifeguard said as he peered down at Ziggy, who opened her bright brown eyes. 'It was kind of you. Some people don't care.'

Ziggy squinted up and raised herself to a sitting position. 'Well, a person's gotta do something,' she said by way of separating herself from some people. 'I thought she was going to have a heart attack.'

'Yeah, she looked a bit rough,' he agreed.

'My Nan keeled over at the beach once. No one came to help her,' Ziggy said desolately. 'I don't get people.'

'Nah, me either.'

Figuring that she was bringing the tone down, she suggested, 'Maybe she was trying to get your attention. She called you Mr Hand-some.'

The lifeguard smiled self-consciously and looked away. 'Mmm,' he mused, 'she's not my type.'

She nearly fell into the trap of asking the lifeguard what his type was.

'So do you come here often?'

'No,' she answered pleasantly, gazing at the horizon.

'Do you normally come to the beach?'

'No,' she teased, 'I don't do anything normally.' Her twinkling eyes rested on his. 'Actually, I usually end up in the cheap seats near the pier with my friends.' She studied his reaction.

'With the normal people,' he conceded.

'Normal? Abnormal? How can you tell?'

It took him a hundred moments to finally ask, 'Um, would you like to meet up for a drink maybe?'

'Mmm, maybe.'

'OK, well, what if I give you my number, and, um, if you want to…'

'So you're willing to take a chance with a girl from the pier?' Ziggy enquired casually, handing him her phone.

'It can't be as frightening as dealing with the girls around here.'

'Foxes, are they?'

'More like wolves.'

After he entered his name and number into Ziggy's phone, he happily handed the phone back saying, 'Awesome, thanks,' and asked her for her name.

'Ziggy. Like in Ziggy Stardust but a girl version.'

'Nah, I don't get it, but I like the name,' he said cheerily.

'Ta…Alex,' she responded as she referred to her phone.

'I think I'm needed back with my offsider, Ziggy. One of those girls might have overdosed on lip gloss. See you soon maybe?'

'Sure. Maybe.'

Ziggy checked her mobile phone before packing it away into her Hello Kitty bag. She took up her towel and dressed and as she passed the grammar school girls, who were at the lifeguard station, she gave a little wave to the lifesaver.

Stepping lightly on the hot sand, she calculated in her head the figure gazillion and one.

Messenger

To wake so early bordered on physical pain, even if it meant escape. When the alarm went off at five in the morning, Sacha pulled the sheet over her tangled copper hair. The repurposed cotton fabric served little in protecting her ears from the digital jangle. She questioned promising Seng that she would pick her up at around six, but she knew Seng, a nurse, would be bobbing around her place like the proverbial cork, accustomed to responding to the call of the ill and ill-at-ease at eccentric hours. Unlike Sacha, who spilled out of bed at eight thirtyish every working day to roll up at Dharma Queens – Ethically Sourced Fashion to facilitate the fulfilment of those tethered to the bondage of retail.

Finally, Sacha reacted to the synthesised squawking by squinting into the dim bedroom and pressing her feet onto the floorboards. The exposure to warm summer air eased her transition from horizontal to vertical.

Sneaking into the kitchen, to avoid waking her housemates, she pulled out a canvas bag of vegetarian nourishment from the fridge and plonked it on the laminex table. As she rammed a muesli bar down her throat and switched the kettle on, she peered through the kitchen window at the faltering starlight and the singed banners of cloud heralding the insurrection of the sun upon night.

Sacha considered that it wasn't so bad to be up at dawn with the breath of Mother Earth in the air. At that moment, she was close to happy. She and Seng had wangled a couple days off work before the New Year. They had both been subjected to the brutality of human excess in the form of Christmas in its various forms and were bound for her family's shack at the coast to heedlessly read bad novels, take guiltless naps and quaff the bulk buy of Grandmother's Organic Pinot obtained from Vinnie, the Preston bottle-o's secret stash. Their only encumbrance was Aden, Sasha's cousin, who was already at the house and due to leave the next day.

The quest for freedom was impeded by hell-bent red lights along Sydney Road and a plague of Melbourne trams. Sacha was running late by the time she got to Dandenong Road. She lurched into the kerb, parking next to Seng, who had been waiting on the nature strip with her backpack on and nibbling rice snacks. She beamed when she saw Sacha speeding down the hill and just about leapt into the car when it stopped. After their greetings, in her haste to get moving, Sasha gunned it out onto the road, cutting off a black Merc. When the driver mouthed a string of abuse, the young women laughed.

Sacha thought it would be bad form to stuff her ears with tissues while Seng played Taylor Swift on her iPad as the old red Toyota belted along the freeway after leaving behind the dreaded Warrigal Road turn-off. Although the lyrics didn't pertain to her exactly, she extracted a sort of subliminal message from the title of the song 'Calm Down'. Her vacuous job was bringing her down and she was exhausted by her bleeding heart activities, as her father disparagingly called them; making anti-Adani signs and badges, writing anti-logging submissions, organising petitions for refugees and picking up rubbish at the canal every Sunday morning. Added to that was the matter of a Centrelink debt which caused her to become despairing and psychopathic in turns with its torrent of faceless threats. She needed a break from it all. She would resist the temptation to turn on the television or read *The Guardian* or Twitter for the next few days.

As they hurtled past the brown paddocks near Nar Nar Goon, the girls were singing/yelling to the cows, 'We're on the road to Hell, Hell, Hell', along with the Northcote girl protest band, No Plastic Bags, from the CD Sasha had skilfully inserted into the player during a lull. The world-weary beasts continued chewing and watching the baffling humans.

Nina Simone was belting out 'Sinnerman' as they drew into the picnic ground and parked beside the weeping willows at Rosedale. The sun was forcing the shadows back and dessicating the bent grass. The girls stood and supped their lattes by the banks of the dwindling Latrobe River.

'Gees, it's starting to get hot already. I can smell smoke, can you?' Sasha asked.

'Um, not really. I can smell gum leaves. It's nice here. I like the trees and the river.'

'I reckon I can smell smoke. It must be from the fire near Bairnsdale.' Sasha pulled the lid off her keep cup and licked the froth off. She continued, 'I don't know how those people in Sydney are coping with that smoke up there day after day. You know, those fires have emitted about half a year of greenhouse gas already.'

Seng nodded.

'Sorry, Sengy, I can't help it.' Sasha apologised, seeing the look on her friend's face.

'It's not that I don't care, Sash, it's just that I'm trying to get from one day to the next.'

'Yeah, I know. I just hope those next days keep coming. Okay, let's hussle.'

Sasha turned to Seng and confessed, 'I've turned my phone off. I don't want to see or hear anything from anyone.'

'Snap. Me too,' Seng admitted with a laugh as she climbed into the car.

The Toyota laboured up the hill on the Princes Highway as the women faced the salt-pan-looking sky. They passed dry paddocks where the cows sought the protection of sparse trees or plugged their feet into dirty, brown dams.

They crossed the Avon River that slipped over silvery river pebbles from the distant mists of Mount Wellington. They followed the highway through the little town of Stratford before passing more paddocks that sprawled to the boundaries of eucalypt forests and the pattern then repeated. The horizon had lost its edge. Everything looked like it was bandaged in gauze.

An electronic road sign flashed up halfway between Stratford and Bairnsdale.

'What was that?' Seng asked, startled out of her sleepy state.

'A warning to be careful about smoke on the road.'

'That's not good,' Seng commented.

'No,' Sasha admitted unsurely, 'but it seems okay here.'

The music had stopped as they got to Lakes Entrance. The red Toyota wheeled around the cliff, revealing the intersection of the four channels that churned gradients of blue and yellow out through the entrance.

Seng cried, 'It's so pretty.'

'Yeah, it's pretty.'

Sasha pulled into the dirt driveway of the fibro shack that stood amongst tall, thin gum trees on a ridge overlooking the ocean.

'Good, Aden's not here. Probably on Bourgeois Des's yacht.'

'What's the go with Aden?'

'Ah, we don't see eye to eye. He's very…um…corporate.'

'…and Bourgeois Des?'

'Desmond Frecklington. He's a snobby high-flyer who's slumming it at Metung when he's not flying to Aspen or Europe for Christmas. We definitely don't get on.'

Bull ants dodged the sparse blades of grass that poked through the dirt.

Seng dropped her backpack in the driveway after she exited the car and stared dreamily at the view. 'It's so nice here. What's down there?' she asked, pointing to where the land dropped away into a chaos of bracken ferns and acacias.

'Not much, just scrub and more trees.'

She wandered down the yard as Sasha followed her. 'Look at this,' she said, inspecting clumps of burnt leaves and ash. 'How sad.'

'It's everywhere,' Sasha exclaimed.

She took up a blackened leaf and examined it closely. Its midrib and veins were raised and defined and its robust texture defied the crucible that brought it to rest here.

'Look at this leaf. It's come kilometres from those fires. I'm keeping this leaf. Look how strong is it; like some sort of tragic, determined messenger. This is our past and our future if we don't do something.'

Inside the house, Sasha picked up a dirty dish from the pile that was in the sink. 'Can you believe he just left this crap here? He's such a pig.'

'Well, I suppose he's on holidays too,' Seng offered.

'Well, so am I,' Sasha snapped and carelessly placed the plate back on the stack.

They dropped their luggage in their rooms. Sasha placed the leaf on her bedside table and then joined Seng, who sat on the deck, taking in the view.

Seng appraised Sasha from where she sat. 'Sash, you look frazzled. You're here to calm down, girl. Can you do it? For a few days, or a few hours or a few minutes? I mean, look where we are. Look at that awesome view. Smell the air. Calm down, my friend.'

'Yes, yes. I know, I know you're right. It just kind of, you know, everything is overwhelming. It's like, people don't behave well. I mean, it's not just Aden leaving mess, it's the whole world, everywhere, the land, the use and abuse. Two hundred years and the place is thoroughly screwed. But yes, you're right. Come on, I'll take you to the entrance and then we can go the beach or have a walk.'

Sasha and Seng perched on a concrete pylon at the end of the sea wall, dangling their legs over the side. Sailing boats drifted past and speedboats coughed along at the restricted speed. Two jet skis sliced through the water, exceeding the speed limit as small craft bobbed in their brash wake. The tourist ferry burbled past as the girls complied with the requisite 'wave to total strangers on passing ferries rule', and the water rattled up the sides of the pylon, wetting their feet. Sasha watched the people with the niggling feeling that everyone was sipping cocktails except her.

They leapt across the gap from the pylon to the sea wall. Sasha landed clumsily in a slurry puddle and almost slipped and fell. Recovering herself, she looked back and noticed more blackened leaves and twigs trailing from the mud as dark as gothic script.

'Are you ready to go to the beach?'

'Yep.'

The women lazily dined and relaxed on the back deck after their long day of travel, swimming and walking. The sun was caramelising in the west, casting burning welts on the sky as it sank.

Sasha put her feet up on a chair and leaned back relishing the mellow effects of alcohol and ocean induced weariness. 'I'm glad to be here, Seng. I hate Christmas and retail,' she said. 'The shop was insane. People were hogging the fitting rooms and one woman was trying on one dress in every colour and it was too small.' She widened her hazel eyes for emphasis. 'I'm not allowed to give advice on size because Giselle, the owner – not her real name, I found out – says it's too sensitive.' She gave an exasperated sigh and raised her eyebrows.

'And then you get the one who comes in five minutes before closing time, when you've had no one in the shop for hours, and they stuff around while you're trying to balance the till and they know it, and then they find, oh my God! exactly what they've been looking for! And you have to be soooo happy for them and stand there with a pleasant smile on your pasty face while they faff about with their maxed-out credit cards, trying to find one that's got some cash on it. And it's getting later and later, and like, you haven't got a life or a home to go to, you know. You'd actually like to catch the bus home before the psychopaths and sex predators come out of the Gleneagles half-cut – like me at the moment.'

Sasha took a swig of Grandmother's Pinot and continued, 'Christmas brings out the worst in me. I could strangle them at times, but I know the minute I went for the jugular, Gisey would swoop on me from behind the kaftan rack or llama wool ponchos where she'd been spying on me through her wayfarers.'

'She sounds not nice.'

'Well, she's all nicey nicey to the customers, but out of the corner of her mouth she's hissing orders like, put the sandalwood beads on the mannequin, hang up the Aztec cardigans, chat to customers, don't chat to them, show them the specials, no show them the new stock, try to be charming, change your face.'

Seng laughed.

'And the clothes are supposed to be ethically sourced and a fair price should be paid to the makers, but honestly some of the mark-ups on the clothes…well, all I can say is that being ethical pays in more ways than one. Her cruelty-free purse is getting nice and fat. I thought it would be a nice place to work while I figure out what I want to do, but I'm jaded.' Sasha poured another Pinot and added, 'I'm too young to be jaded, Sengy, too young.'

'Ha ha. Yeah, I know. I'm so over everything too. On Monday, I finished my shift which was manic, I ride out of the car park and I see this sad individual, high as a – I don't know, like that big tree over there – and he was wandering all over the street and then he just walked straight out into traffic. Bang! Straight into a car. Well, what do you do? So over I go. He's like, "Whoa, what happened?" and he's totally relaxed, except he says his neck hurts a bit. He looks up at me and says, "What's with that guy?" because the driver's shitting his pants and screaming. I really felt like running away, because I'd been on my feet for ten hours, but I had my uniform on, so it would have been a really bad look for me to hop on my bike and take off with everyone around. So I ring for an ambulance because he needs to be checked out and he could have a spinal injury because he's still on his back and he's got a sore neck. And cars are tooting and more people are milling around, and then he sits up and starts swearing at me because I've rung for an ambulance! "Oh, you slanty-eyed bitch, what are you effin' ringin' them for? I'm not effin' goin' with them, they just wanna effin' lock me up, blah, blah, blah." And the driver's hyperventilating and some people are filming it all on their phones. What heroes.'

'Oh my God, that's awful. I hate Australia sometimes.'

'Well, I don't hate Australia. At least here the military don't shoot at your grandfather, or burn your parents' church down and make you flee your home. But yeah, some people are a bit out of control.'

Sasha felt the reigns being pulled on her galloping indignation on behalf of Seng about the racial slur. Through Seng's lens, Sasha caught sight of the quicksilver flash of light and shadow that stage lit the life of a refugee. Her own problems faded, but her *Weltschmerz* remained.

For minutes, the women sat without words, listening to the restless sea and frantic mozzies.

Finally, Sasha said, 'Yeah…people are pigs.' Then she added, 'Speaking of which, here comes Aden,' as the sound of tyres was heard on the driveway.

'Should I expect him to be rude to me?' Seng asked jokingly.

'Oh no, he won't be rude to you, but he will be rude to me.'

Aden appeared at the back deck greeting the women.

'Hello, Aden.' Sasha performed the introductions flatly. 'This is my friend Seng. Seng, this is my cousin Aden.'

'Hi, Sang, nice to meet you.' Aden said, offering his hand.

'Seng, Aden. Seng.' Sasha corrected him irritably.

'Sorry. Seng. Hard to hear Sash when she mumbles,' Aden explained with a grin and a wink.

'I don't mumble,' Sasha replied and as an aside commented to Seng. 'It's just that he only understands weasel words.'

'Sash says that's the language I use in my job. She doesn't like my line of business, I'm in marketing, sorry to say, Seng. But in a sense, Sash and I really both want the same thing. We both want to persuade-people's opinions and clean up, eh, Sash?' He nudged her into recognising his witticism and she obliged with a pained look.

'So what have you ladies been up to today? I see you've enjoyed some refreshments,' Aden observed, inspecting the bottle. 'Do you mind?'

'Go for it, but I doubt it'll be up to your standard,' Sasha said.

Aden pursed his lips. 'Ooh – a bit bitey. So I didn't expect you to be here.'

'Why?'

'Well, the fires and the warnings.'

'What do you mean?'

'Didn't you get the text messages?'

'What text messages?'

'Well, the ones basically telling you to go the hell back to Melbourne.'

Sasha and Seng looked at one another in horror as Aden showed the messages to the women from his phone. The shocking warnings alarmed them as they scrolled through. 'You are in danger…Bairnsdale to Cann River. If you don't leave today, road closures are likely to mean that you are unlikely to get home. Lakes Entrance: if you are holidaying in this part of the state, it's recommended you leave this part of the state NOW.'

He tapped the Emergency Services app as the screen populated with images of black flames in diamonds.

'Oh my God, we'll have to leave. Right now.'

'Cool your jets, cuz, you're here now. I've just come back from Metung and it was fine. This fire is a fair way north of the highway. It's not going to race up here in ten minutes. And that one at Buchan – well, you know how far Buchan is. And those are watch and act.'

'Yeah, but look what it says. Obviously emergency services don't want stupid idiots here if shit gets real.'

'Yeah, but I don't think they'd want people driving into the night after a skinful either.'

'But it's selfish to stay. You shouldn't be here. We're just in the way if we have to be evacuated.'

'We won't need evacuating tonight and, to be honest, Sash, Seng looks like she might be able to handle the wheel, but I wouldn't get in a car with you. You look like you're about to roll under the table. What do you think, Seng?'

'To be honest, I'd really like to go home and be safe, but sorry, Sash, I think we'd better hunker down tonight. I think Aden is right.'

Sasha addressed Aden. 'Thanks for undermining me in front of my friend, Aden.' She then turned to Seng. 'I'm so sorry, Seng. What a horrible thing to do to you. Jesus I hope we'll be okay.'

'We will be okay,' Aden said.

'How do you know that?' Sasha asked angrily and then checked herself, trying to assure Seng as well as herself. 'We will be okay.' With that, she swiped the wine from the table, put her arm around Seng and said, 'I'm going inside. The mosquitoes are bugging me. And that's not the only thing that's bugging me.'

They entered the house, where they threw themselves down on the couch. Sasha switched the television on.

Catching the late news, the screen filled with men in dark uniforms, making pleas, demands and warnings with dry mouths, enunciating heavy words about fires breaching containment lines, winds and crews working through the night as the autocue rolled grimly on. Shoulders flanked shoulders in high-ranking support. Camera footage showed the horror of flames devouring forests, and tearing through farms and lashing fire trucks.

'I'm sorry, Sengy,' Sasha said.

'I'm okay, this situation isn't your fault,' Seng replied, although Sasha didn't hear her as she fell asleep on the couch.

Seng had prepared a ginger tea and was on her way out the back door, when Sasha opened her eyes.

'Sengy,' Sasha whispered, trying not to wake Aden.

'Morning, Sash. I'll get you a cup.'

They scurried onto the back deck cradling their teas. The northerly was stirring and carrying smoke. They watched the thin slice of light on the horizon on the verge splitting the day apart.

'Thanks, Seng, I needed that. It's so smoky and creepy out here. I'm glad we're going back today. These fires are breaking out everywhere and forty degrees and wind today aren't going to help,' Sasha said as she rested her cup on the table.

'I wonder if there's anything that we can do to help here?'

'I wondered that too.'

'How are you feeling?'

'I've been better – I'm not used to drinking much. I'll be happy to go home.'

'I feel ill, but I don't know if it's because I've had too much to drink, being worried about you, seeing the horrible carnage or having Aden here.'

'He's not so bad.'

'What?'

'Well, you flaked and we chatted. He's nice. Oh, and he brought out some really good wine to try.'

'Oh really?' Sasha raised her eyebrow, bemused. 'So you were holding out on me.'

Seng turned, swallowed down her tea and tossed the dregs to the garden.

'And don't worry about me. It's you you should be worried about. Do you want some breakfast?'

'Ugh, don't even talk about it.'

Sasha and Seng had packed their bags and started to clean up when Aden entered the kitchen, giving a perfunctory wave as he spoke on his phone.

'So you're doing what? Are you sure? Do you need someone with you? I'll come down and help. OK. I'll catch you down there.' Aden frowned. 'Des is insane.'

'Ahuh,' Sasha agreed as she gave Aden a quizzical look.

'He's taking the yacht around to Mallacoota.'

'What?'

'His mate and mother are there. He thinks he might be able to get them onto the boat. The road is closed to Gippsland and the mum isn't super well.'

'Say what? Des?' Sasha screwed up her face. 'I didn't know he had it in him.'

'Yeah I know. He's going to the supermarket in town to get water and bread and tins of stuff in case people need it. He doesn't have a clue.'

'I'll help him,' Sasha announced. 'I have to do something.'

'That's what he said: "I have to do something."'

By the jetty, Sasha was dancing in the conga line with Seng and Aden as Bruno Mars warbled 'Count on Me' from the old CD player as supplies were relayed to Des, who was below deck.

'Over there. Over there,' Sasha barked to Des from above the hatch as she spied a space to store the last of the goods.

The conga line stopped and the music was turned down as the group gathered on the jetty for farewells.

Sasha held Aden by the shoulders and told him to drive extra carefully. She hugged Seng tightly. 'You're right, he's not so bad.'

Des tapped his foot impatiently, stepped onto the yacht, slotted another CD into the player and announced that it was time to go.

The boat drifted away from the jetty.

'Are you scared?' Sasha called above the wind to Des.

'Petrified,' he admitted nervously.

They laughed hysterically when Sasha cried, 'Me too.'

Sasha's feet were planted boldly on the deck of the yacht. She pulled out the burnt leaf and held it up for a moment. Its fluttering pulsed urgently in her fingertips before she carefully slid it back into her pocket. They were propelled onward and into the hurtling currents and dreadful depths. The notes of Pink Floyd's 'On the Turning Away' climbed upon the wind as they bounced through the entrance and left the protective arm of the lake.

www.ingramcontent.com/pod-product-compliance
Lightning Source LLC
Chambersburg PA
CBHW030821200726
48288CB00004B/1330